A Simple Hello

A Hot New Romance Series Based on a True Story

SARAH LOUISE ROSMOND

ISBN: 9781999900113

Cover designed and created by the author

First published in the United Kingdom in 2017 where the author used her original birth name.

Republished 2018 under the name of Sarah Louise Rosmond.

ELLA & TYLOR

Contents

ACKNOWLEDGMENTS

Firstly, I would like to thank my family who without them I would never have put pen to paper. A big massive thank you to my partner who has endured nights where I have been clearly frying his head with little snippets and ideas for this book, and a thank you to my children who have let me have the time in the evenings that I have needed to create this book. Without my family, none of this would have ever been possible. They have believed in me from the start.

I would also like to thank my cousin and my uncle who have both become my proof readers and editors. We love each other to bits but neither of them has ever been scared to tell me if a plot isn't working or if something isn't sitting right with my characters. Their honesty can only improve my writing.

Like most writers I spend a lot of time at home in front of my keyboard and I would like to thank my few close friends who have accepted that my time is limited, and their support has spurred me on to get my work out there.

Most of all I would like to thank my readers, without you this dream of mine, would never have come true. I thank you from the bottom of my heart for your continued support and ongoing loyalty xoxo

SR xo

CHAPTER ONE…

Well where do I start?

Let's go back to the very beginning, then, shall we?

Well my name is Elouise Jayne Roberts, but I really cannot stand my full name, it reminds me of my childhood, the times when you knew you were in deep trouble.

Nowadays everyone refers to me as Ella.

So maybe I should explain a little about myself? Well I don't really know what to tell you, apart from that I am almost 30 years old and very much single again with no children and I work for someone who drains the life out of me and in all honestly, Stacey's shop just reminds me of everything I have lost. Depressing I know, but don't despair as life is about to get a whole lot more interesting, but first you get to meet the more cantankerous side to me…

It is Tuesday morning and I am rudely awoken by my alarm ringing in my ear, I swear I have not long fallen to sleep. That has me in a lovely mood I can assure you. I don't want to move as I peel my body from my lovely warm bed, into the instant freeze which is my one bed flat. As I am leaning over my bed to grab my dressing gown, shivering and trying to stop my teeth from chattering together, I end up stumping my big toe on the foot of the bed.

Why is everything so bloody stressful lately?

Well I would tell you, if I even knew a reason myself.

I barely have the motivation to do anything this past few weeks, which really isn't like me at all.

I am usually very upbeat and positive. If something is bothering me I would normally let it slide, opting for a peaceful life.

I have been accused of being too soft and a push over at times but that's not the case, I just like to make my days as easy as possible. It sounds a bit weak and pathetic I know but I hate any type of confrontation, so if I can be calm and polite in everything I do, then I am usually happy enough, but not lately. Lately I am just so God damn fed up and feel like I want to snap. I can't seem to muster up the excitement for anything in my life and I can assure you that is not a good thing if my past is anything to go by.

I suppose I best get myself ready for work.

I work in a small gift shop in the quiet annex of the market hall. It is a little disheartening really, because it was less than a year ago when I had my own business. My own shop was just around the corner on Regent Street and stocked similar new aged gifts to Stacey's stall.

I was lucky enough to be based in a busy enough location on the outskirts of the town centre, with a lot of passing trade and I was in my element. Until one day my whole business went up in flames, literally. It was all due to an electrical fault but being naïve and thinking I would never need it, I hadn't got around to renewing my public liability insurance. As you can imagine, this left me with nothing to show for seven years of arduous work.

I wouldn't mind going into work as much if it wasn't a Tuesday. Stacey is in today, she is the owner of the shop but when she is at work the day seems to drag out a little longer than normal. Unlike her Sister Kathy who will chat all day long; Stacey likes to bury her head into a book and just sit at the back of the shop, glancing up every so often, as if she needs to babysit me.

There are some serious trust issues with her I think, but she would never say anything to my face. I can just tell by the way she is always checking the till and making sure it all tally's up in her books. I have never stolen a thing in my life and I try my hardest not to take it as a personal insult but if she starts today I may just snap and say something.

It is quarter to nine and I'm stood outside in the pouring rain and Stacey nowhere to be seen. We are meant to be open by now so that we have time to set the stall up and I wouldn't mind as much normally, but I am going to look like a drowned rat at this rate, why didn't I put my other coat on? I give myself a mental telling off, but I know why I didn't grab my coat, it looked lovely and sunny less than half an hour ago. I really should know by now; how unpredictable the English weather is, but I am ever the optimist.

Finally, she is here, only twenty-five minutes late today, she is the owner of this business and I feel she should be setting me an example, although I am not cheeky enough to voice my opinions to her.

'Good morning Elouise' Stacey is far too chirpy today and it grates on me.

I try and greet her with the same enthusiasm but even I can tell I sound like I am forcing every single bit of it. Luckily for me, Stacey is a little dimmer than most and doesn't seem to notice my sarcasm. Not that she would say anything to me if she did. I don't see why either. I am far from a scary woman, standing less than 5ft tall and slim built I couldn't see anyone fearing me, to be honest. I just think it is the way this woman is, and I get that.

If anything, ever has needed to be said to her employees then Stacey would always ask her Sister to take over the helm. Stacey loves the idea of owning her own shop, but if you ask me she still has a lot to learn, but at least she pays for her public liability insurance. I think telling her about my own mistake made her realise how important the insurance is.

The shop has been dead most of the day and I honestly feel like I am wasting my time here.

I feel like this most days lately and I have lost every ounce of enthusiasm in this job, but today is just dragging in longer than normal.

I could probably get away with leaving early but I don't see the point as I wouldn't be doing much at home either.

I keep telling myself that I may as well earn a few extra quid. Although I do need to do something, sitting in this shop listening to James Blunt all day, has me wanting to fall asleep. I don't mind his music in small doses, but Stacey absolutely loves a bit of Blunt, the only time I have ever seen her get excited was a few months back when Kathy had managed to get hold of two tickets to go and see him live, she was like a child at Christmas. Since then we have listened to his album on repeat every Tuesday and Friday without fail and I can sing ever lyric to you by memory.

'Stacey, is there anything I can do? I ask.

I really am bored shitless, but I can't really go and say that to her without offending the poor woman.

'Can I arrange the stock or tidy up maybe?'

I already know she will say no, but I ask her anyway.

Stacey turns to look at me, raising her eyebrow and placing her index finger at the line of the story that I have clearly interrupted her from. She can get rather moody if you mess up her reading flow as I found out the first week I started here.

'No, it's okay, I did it all over the weekend, why not read or something' she smiles looking back down at the fingered page.

I am frustrated now, she knows fine rightly that I had my own shop like this for years, hence why she employed me in the first place. Yet she cannot trust me to do anything but sit behind this stupid till for six hours straight. I ask if I can go outside for a smoke and to stretch my legs. Stacey agrees without lifting her head to look at me.

I don't know why I even wasted my breath asking her anything because last week, when I was in on my own, I had decided to tidy up anyway, just around the main till area. Honestly, you should have seen her face that afternoon when she got back. Not only that, but the fact it looks just as messy again only a few days later says it all.

I want to say something about my need to do more than just sit in the same spot for six hours, but I don't say a word. Instead I start to look through her pile of fantasy romance novels. Not really the type of book I would read but each to their own. I love a good thriller, but I have become lazy lately and would opt for watching the movie if I can, rather than reading a book.

Standing outside having a smoke, and I get a text off my best friend Jude. I have just remembered I told her I would pop in for a coffee before heading home but with the way today has been I am wishing I hadn't. I really need to go otherwise she will be on the warpath like last time.

Jude is one of my eldest friends but with that comes my most pushy and somewhat overprotective friend too. I love her, but she can be very over bearing with her opinions and times and has been doing my head a little more than normal lately, droning on about how I need to start going out more and that I need to find myself a guy.

The last thing I want in my life at the minute is a man, but she doesn't listen, Jude always knows best of course.

I know our coffee chat is just to probe me about the guy I met up with over the weekend. Jude had been a match maker with a friend of a friend and I only agreed really, out of curiosity. His name was Darren, but he was a lot older than me and had a weird smell about him, I knew within the first five minutes that it wasn't going anywhere so after we had both finished eating, I had politely excused myself and made my escape, paying my half of the tab on the way out. Darren was still sat at the table waiting on me, but something about him made me feel uneasy so I didn't feel guilty, even though I maybe thought I should.

Stacey is huffing and puffing while packing the unit back up.

'Been a long day eh?' I say as she's locking the front door.

'Things will pick up, it's just the time of year' she says, almost as if she is defending herself.

'Oh, don't worry, I know what it is like' I try and say it as reassuring as I can and of course I have to add a cheeky reminder of my own experience with a gift shop.

I can at least be grateful that it isn't raining anymore and the walk to Jude's is quite refreshing, which I am grateful for because half an hour ago, I could have easily fallen straight to sleep.

I have to say I am intrigued to know what has Jude looking so unnaturally happy today. I have seen her Facebook status saying that she has some exciting news, but she hasn't mentioned what it is, or at least she hasn't said anything online, and Jude would normally love to gloat on social media.

We are sat at the kitchen table when I smile at her.

'So, tell me what has put such a big smile on your face?' I ask.

'Oh, you know' she says too casually.

'No, I don't but you're going to tell me' I say, raising my eyebrow and giving her the all-knowing look.

'Okay, well Dan asked me to marry him last night'

I squint a little at the pitch of her voice, clearly one very excited Jude. I am so happy for her and tell her to stand up, so I can give her a big hug in congratulations.

That has made my pointless day seem a lot more worthwhile now, and it is about time too. Dan and Jude have been together for as long as I can remember, and they have a six-year-old daughter together, marriage was clearly the next step, but Dan has been telling Jude for the past two years that he loves her, but he will never marry her. One evening about two years ago now, Jude was set to end the whole relationship because he had said this to her. Jude took it out of context and seen it as Daniel telling her that she wasn't good enough for him in some way. It was hard bloody work calming her down with that one. Jude can become very ridged and fixed in her ideas and it takes a lot to convince that woman, that she may in fact, be wrong.

I think seeing Jude so happy with her little family unit has made me a little jealous lately. Not jealous of her or anything like that, but just a little downhearted about my own pointless life. It seems like everyone else I have ever known, has either been off making babies or at least making something of themselves. I am almost 30 years old and I have nothing to show for it, apart from a few pounds I have saved in the hope to move away one day. I honestly have nothing here, and that is starting to get me down the most lately.

I have wanted to move away for a while now and after talking to my Mum on the phone for the past few weeks, I have decided to go over to Belfast for a while and see what it can offer me, because I can tell you something, for nothing, living in Manchester hasn't seemed to work out too well, so far.

I used to live on the outskirts of Belfast as a child, off and on, but can't ever remember visiting the city itself. I am sure I did at some point, but I am guessing I was very young at the time. Mum raves on about how much I would love it there every week when I call her, but I have never really taken much notice up until today.

I am feeling down in the dumps and just want my Mum.

Seeing Jude beaming with happiness makes me realise how everyone that is everyone, is getting on with their lives. So why the hell haven't I? Something needs to change and so I decide to look online at prices, I am soon starting to plan my trip away, and sooner, rather than later.

Travelling to Belfast is a lot cheaper than what I had expected, which kind of makes me wonder why I haven't been over to see my Mum sooner. A tiny prang of guilt hits me, but I know it works both ways and I am always the one who rings her first.

Why am I even trying to defend myself?

Yes, so as you may have guessed, we have a slight Mummy issue going on here. Not really in a bad way like my Mother was never mean to me or anything, it is just that I seemed to fade into the background growing up and it hasn't ever bothered me but being the eldest of eight other siblings, I did get the brunt of it most of the time. I won't even get into the story with my dad but let's just say my mother let him do whatever he wanted, just to get an easy life. I can only imagine how hard it must have been for her while we were growing up. The thought of one baby scares the crap out of me, never mind eight arguing, fighting noisy snotty kids. With all that stress, simple tasks would soon turn into a lot of heated arguments with us all.

I would get told off and smacked for things I hadn't even done. Although, being the way, I am; I found it easier to own up and take the punishment that was set, rather than to have to sit and witness the arguments and fowl moods for hours on end, just because someone else had refused to own up to it themselves. I am still a little like that nowadays, I will say sorry even if I don't think I am in the wrong and it is usually Jude I am apologizing to.

Maybe that's where my hatred towards confrontation comes from. Who knows?

I like the fact that I come across as gentle and a little timid at times. Most of that also comes with the fact that I'm not much taller than a child. Apparently, it makes me cuter being smaller than the average adult, but I can tell you it's not all that fun. Especially if you're trying to pull off sexy and end up coming across as all cute and innocent instead.

Not that I have felt sexy or even had a sexual relationship in such a long time anyway. I'm not complaining, and I do love being single, but it does get lonely sometimes and maybe that's why seeing Jude all happy and settling down has made me a little envious tonight.

I have paid for my tickets and rang Mum to confirm everything; now all that is left to do is, tell Jude.

I'm sure she will be happy for me, she did after all mention to me at Christmas that I should go over and see my Mum and younger siblings but with working in a gift shop it meant I had no time for much else. I think about just sending Jude a text message, but I would be well pissed off if she were to just text me to say she was leaving so I give my head a wobble and get myself ready to make my way to my best friend's house.

I decide to take the short cut and find myself walking past the market, all I can say is thank God it is a Wednesday today, because Stacey doesn't open shop on a Wednesday or Thursday as she says the days drag and the market is quiet, the place is dead most days but I am not complaining, working in that shop four days a week is more than enough for me!

I have planned to tell Stacey on Friday morning that I am moving away and therefore handing in my notice, I know it isn't much time as I am leaving on Sunday, but I need to get out of here as soon as possible, now that I have set my mind to it. Although I can't quite tell if I am nervous or excited yet and I have a sicky feeling in the pit of my stomach.

I am very nervous about telling Jude now that I am here. My friend thinks I have just come for our regular catch up, but it has just dawned on me how much I am going to miss her.

I can feel my eyes starting to well up, but I somehow manage to contain myself when she answers her front door, she smiles and leads me into the kitchen to offer me a cup of tea.

Jude is nattering away about some old man cutting her up with a trolley when she stops and looks at me.

'What's up?' she asks, instantly putting the lyrics from the 90s hit at the forefront of my mind.

'I'm going to see my Mum for a while' I bite the bottom of my lip trying to look regretful, I am regretful though.

Telling my best friend that I won't see her for a while isn't as easy as you might think or wasn't as easy as I had hoped it would be. Jude however tries to make me feel a bit better about my decision and even seems a little excited for me.

'Pity I wouldn't fit in your suitcase' she laughs doing her famous snort as she catches her breath. Even her snort I will miss.

CHAPTER TWO…

I cannot sleep for the life of me.

It is three in the morning and I am wide awake.

What the hell! My flight isn't till midday and it only takes forty minutes on the plane, so I wasn't planning on waking up till at least eight but now I am clearly wide awake, and I may as well get up and make sure my suitcase is all packed. I already know it is, because I checked it before I went to bed, but I will amuse myself and check it one more time. Just to be on the safe side.

Once I know everything is ready I make my way to the sofa and reach down the side to retrieve the remote. I will be surprised if I can find anything to watch at this ridiculous time of the night, but I need to do something to switch off my brain.

Shit! I must have drifted off as I am awoken by my alarm going off from up the stairs, shit! I look at the clock its almost nine o clock.

My alarm has clearly been going off for the past hour. Why didn't I bring my phone downstairs?!

Once I am washed and dressed, I calm down a little, I still have over two hours before my flight, but I know if I had any sense at all, I would leave soon because knowing my luck traffic will be an absolute nightmare.

As usual I am right, the traffic is horrendous this morning. I wouldn't mind but even though we are stuck behind other vehicles the meter is still running and I am starting to think that I should have walked to the airport instead.

At this rate, I will miss my flight and this stupid taxi will cost me more than the plane ticket! I think the taxi driver can sense my urgency and has apologised a few times now. Doesn't stop him charging me an arm and a leg, though does it? I still smile politely to him and tell him that it's okay and not his fault, which it isn't. Now, if I had of needed a taxi in the morning or late afternoon, I would have been fine, but traffic is always bad up until two-ish.

I only just manage to check in even though I left with plenty of time to spare and that taxi ride must have been the longest trip to the airport ever! It even set me back over twenty-seven pounds. I am not impressed, considering the last time I got a taxi here, it was less than half the price. I honestly cannot wait to see the back of Manchester.

I already miss Jude, but I must admit that she is probably one of the only things I will miss about this place.

I do wonder though what Belfast will be like? It is a city after all and I never guessed I would use my savings to move to yet another city. I had always imagined that I would end up in a lovely rural cottage in the country side, but my mother assures me that Belfast is a small city. I did have a quick glance at google maps last night and Manchester seems massive in comparison.

One thing my mother did warn me about was the weather, she says that it gets bitterly cold in the winter. I may have to stock up on some warmer winter clothing when I get there because most of the things in that small suitcase of mine, are made from thin, flimsy material. I don't even think I have another jumper packed apart from the one tied around my waist. It looked a lot duller outside when I left the house earlier, but as always, looks can be deceiving and the sun is out in all its glory now.

I find a seat by the waiting area and retrieve my book from my backpack. I have about half an hour before they start boarding so I am guessing I can at least squeeze another chapter in. I am slightly engrossed in this book, well in all honesty I thought it would take my mind off things if I can escape into an enjoyable book.

It kind of did, as the story was about taking risks and how it is better to be disappointed than to never know what could have been.

I can relate to that so much at the minute.

I think that's what makes an enjoyable book, when it is something you can relate to in some way.

We are starting to board the plane and I can feel my little heartbeat start to race as I make my way towards the back of the plane and take my seat.

This is always the worst part, isn't it?

Just as the engines start up and the plane starts to coast down the runway. I can feel the ends of my fingers stinging but I refuse to release my grip on the arm rest. I think I have watched far too much air scene investigations shows and that has me feeling a little paranoid.

A few more seconds and we will be up in the air and all will be fine.

Fuck me, this must be the longest few seconds of my life. It could be worse though. The older gentleman sat beside me has his eyes tightly shut and looks like he is about to combust, all red faced and sweaty.

Is it bad that seeing someone more terrified than me has calmed me down immensely?

Go me! I even let go of the armrests in record time.

Normally the cold worn leather gets my attention for more than a few seconds at a time. It's more like a good few minutes before I feel comfortable enough to let go, seeing this man so scared beside me has honestly made me realise how silly I, myself, must look.

'This is the worst of it' I say as reassuring as I can to the man just as he opens his eyes and catches me staring at him.

I kind of want to hug him but in the same breath, I am ever so slightly amused about how scared he seems.

'Is this your first time?' I ask wondering why on earth anyone would put themselves through this ordeal more than is necessarily needed.

'Oh, no' he replied, his voice a little shaky 'I take this plane every month or so to visit my family back home'.

I can hear the Irish accent instantly.

I smiled at the man before telling him that I am moving over to Belfast for a while and that I am going to stay with my Mum. The man goes on to tell me all about Belfast, where the best museums and galleries are, and how lovely it generally is over there. I can't help but wonder why he didn't just stay in Ireland, and being a nosey cow, I had to ask him.

'My wife passed away a few years ago, and she is buried in Chester where we lived together so I can't leave her behind, I take this plane all the time, but the flight never gets any easier.'

I feel so sorry for him.

If I am to guess his age I would say he was in his early fifties and in my eyes far too young to be a widower. I didn't really know what to say after that.

'Life can be cruel' I say looking at the floor.

'It can be, but it can also be wonderful' I look up and the man is smiling now.

'I had over thirty years with the most amazing woman on this earth, and I feel privileged because not everyone is as lucky to find love as I have been'

I smile and ask the man his name. he introduces himself as George.

'I am Ella, very pleased to meet you' I say shaking George's hand.

'Well Ella, if you have that special person you can truly connect with, then never let them go, no matter what'

I explain that I don't and sadly believe I will never be lucky enough to find true love and how I do wonder if it even exists nowadays. My past relationships have been very controlling and definitely not made from love. They have all started off well and good, but within a year or so, they have all shown their true colours.

'Oh, it does, I think that if you ever meet this person you will know straight away, they will blow your mind and I hope that you will think back to this conversation in years to come' he has a big smile on his face at this point and I don't want to burst his positive bubble so I just smile back at him.

'I really hope you are right George'

CHAPTER THREE...

My Mum has arrived to meet me at the airport. She said she was worried about me getting on the wrong bus into the city and even though I told her that I would be fine, I am still kind of glad she is here. I give her a hug and make a comment about her new hair colour. It is black with red high lights and looks good on her, I would even go as far to say that it makes her look a little younger.

I manage to talk her into having a coffee at Starbucks with me before we get a taxi to hers. I just want ten minutes with my mother before entering the mad house, which is her home.

Izabelle and Benjamin are my youngest of siblings and by a long shot the most spoilt. From what Mum has told me on the phone they are both a handful and her house can be crazy from eight in the morning until eight at night.

It is only coming up to four o'clock and I am sure she won't let me keep her here for another four hours.

Twenty minutes or so will have to do for now. It is lovely because my Mum really does seem excited to see me, as I am with her.

Once we arrive at my Mum's house it is obvious that my Brother and Sister are both very excited to see me. Izzy came running towards me, almost knocking me off my feet as soon as she seen the taxi pull up outside.

'Wow, you are getting big' I stated, noticing that she is at least a foot taller than I remember.

Her hair has lightened too whereas before, it looked more like a deep brown and now it's a light mousy blonde. I asked Mum if she has dyed my little Sister's hair, but she assures me that it has just lightened in the sunshine.

'I have missed you' she replies before wrapping her arms around my waist.

Ben just stands by the door and smiles at me.

He is almost twelve now so totally uncool to give his big Sister a hug. I make my way over to the doorway and manage to rummage my hand through his perfectly styled hair.

'Do not touch the hair' he snaps trying to protect his head from my dreaded hand, but it doesn't work as I still manage to mess up his locks.

I heard him call me a bitch as he walks away muttering under his breath, but I choose to ignore it and make my way into the kitchen where my Mum is now standing.

'Fancy a coffee?' she asks but I think I am only functioning this week due to the amount of caffeine I drink lately, so I shake my head.

'I'm okay for now but thank you anyway Mum'.

This case of mine isn't exactly light, so I ask where I can put it and I am told that I am sharing Izzy's room with her. My excited nine-year-old Sister has just started screeching behind me.

'I will show you were our room is'.

I can't help but laugh as she tries to help with my case and can't even manage to lift it off the floor.

'It's okay Izzy I can get it' I say with a smile.

I didn't really know what to expect from a nine-year olds bedroom, but I am pleasantly surprised when I see that Izzy has tried to partition off the room a little.

Her half of the room is full of teddies and toys all piled neatly in the corners and over her bed whereas the side of the room I guess is mine, has been cleared for my arrival. You can see that I am in a little girl's bedroom with pink fairies all over the wall, but Mum told me she had bought a new bedding set for me as she guessed I didn't want to sleep with unicorns or fairies.

Talking about my Mum, I can hear her coming up the stairs.

'Your Sister has been up here all morning making her room tidy for you'.

I look at Izzy and smile, before brushing her long blonde hair from her face and kissing her forehead.

'Thank you, sweetheart'

'I even emptied the drawers' she said pointing to the vanity table by my bed 'so you have somewhere to put your clothes' My Baby Sister smiles at me.

'She even cleared out that old unit of yours Ella, just so you have somewhere to put all your makeup and perfumes' Mum explains.

'That is so kind of you both, thank you Mum'

'No need to thank me, you are my little girl too. No matter how old you get' she smiles before walking back out of the room, Izzy following behind her.

A few seconds later my Mum appears in the doorway again.

'I got these towels last week especially' she says passing me three neatly folded towels of varied sizes. 'we got you lilac, so you knew which were for you'

'I have pink ones and Mum has white. Benji has blue ones' Izabelle says peeping her head back around the door frame.

I feel a little weirded out but not in a bad way. Mum seems so much calmer than I remember and a lot more organised than she was when I was a small child, but I suppose when I was younger there was a lot more of us living in the house and a lot more always going on.

After I unpacked most of my belonging, I noticed Izzy made her way back up the stairs to me and offers to help me arrange my only perfume onto the side and the small contents of my makeup bag onto the vanity unit which she cleared especially for me. Once we have completed our short task, we make our way back down stairs. Izzy all happy that she has been able to help me.

Mum, Izzy and myself sit down in the living room.

I am grateful Mum had made me a cup of tea while I was sorting the last of my things out. Though I do need to ask for it a little stronger next time.

In my opinion, there is nothing worse than a milky cup of tea, but this one is drinkable at least.

My Mother is on her phone and Izzy is glued to Victorious. I am finding myself just as engrossed but I'm not really watching the tv, my mind is elsewhere while my eyes are fixed on the box in the corner of the room.

I hear Mum giggle which brings me out of my trance.

She looks up just as I look in her direction.

'I have just been asked out on a date with a man that's half my age' she says blushing.

I dart over to the other sofa and I'm almost sat on her lap, eager to see the message.

'That's awesome Mum, you should definitely go' I say excited for her.

'Don't be silly, look at me'

My Mum is almost fifty and I think it is getting her down a bit, but she has nothing to worry about, she has always had the benefit of looking younger than her actual age. Most likely where I have inherited it from.

'Mum don't be stupid. I will have the kids while you have a much-needed night out' she didn't look convinced. 'even if it amounts to nothing, at least you can have a good night out'.

'I will think about it' she looks all down hearted.

'Here' she says as if she had just had the best idea in the world.

'Why don't we make you a profile?' her eyes widened and dart straight at me. I really do not like the sound of this.

'No Mum, I'm not sure internet dating is for me'

She looks really gutted and then goes on to explain how much she enjoys the attention and the nice messages off handsome men and that it didn't mean I had to go on dates. After over an hour of talking about this site, she has finally convinced me. Perhaps a little attention would be nice, it's not like I had to meet anyone after all.

Taking over my phone, the woman looked like she is in her element, I honestly haven't seen my mother so elated than she is now and it makes me smile.

'I need to add some photos of you' she explains wanting to look through my gallery on my phone.

'I don't have many recent ones' and I really don't, I think the last photo taken of me on my phone was over two years ago.

I have recent photos on my Facebook but that's only in group photos that I have been tagged in and not ones I would like to use for any dating sites.

What the hell have I let myself in for? I think to myself.

I would never have dreamt about internet dating before today, and now Mum has me slightly excited about creating this account.

'It's okay, we can update them afterwards' she says with a huge smile of her face.

'I love this one of you' she says looking at a photo taken of me over five years ago.

'Yes, but I don't look like that anymore' I say concerningly.

The photograph in question is one of me standing on a beach in a black flowing top. It is so sunny that the ocean is glistening behind me. My hair looks a warm ginger colour from the glow of the sunlight and has half covered my face as it had been windy that day.

'I do look good in this photo, and it is the best one of me so far, but like I said it is over five years old now and really doesn't look like me anymore'

'Yes, it does, your hair is just darker now' she says defending herself as she adds it to my profile anyway.

'Think it should be your main profile picture?' Mum has said like she is waiting for me to agree.

'Has that not got a name?' I ask but she just looks back at me with a confused expression to her face.

'What do you mean?'

I am sure I have read somewhere that people on these types of sites tend to use a photo that looks nothing like themselves to bag a date. Cat fishing or something I think it is called.

'Mum you can't use that one, I don't want to be branded as a catfish now do I?' I explain my concerns.

'You are being silly, it still looks like you, because it is you!' she states.

She is right after all, it is me just a few years younger, so I eventually give in and allow her to set it as my profile picture.

A few minutes pass while my Mum is typing away on my screen.

'It's all done now' she sounds very proud of herself as she passes me back my phone.

'You might want to read the write up about yourself' she looks at me and waves her cup.

'Tea?'

'Yes please, a little less milk though' I reply remembering the milkier cup I had been given earlier.

She makes her way out to the kitchen while I cautiously read what she has written on my profile.

To be fair to her my Mum has wrote a good paragraph about me, it's not too self-absorbed but it does make me sound very interesting. I suppose I am a little interesting after all. I play the guitar, though I do not claim to do it very well, it is still something that I enjoy doing.

I am creative and enjoy drawing and painting but again I am very modest and wouldn't have necessary wrote this about myself. I am glad my Mum has taken over, because I don't think I would have known what to write about and even though I enjoy reading and writing about other people, I had never tried writing about myself. I even needed help with my curriculum vitae when I was seeking employment because apparently, I didn't come across confident enough.

I place my phone down and make my way into the kitchen where Mum is stood looking at her own device.

Then one of them starts pinging straight away, Mum tells me that it is my phone because hers is on silent.

'I know that sound, you have a message on that site already'

'I have three apparently' I respond picking my phone up from the arm of the chair.

I open my phone which locks itself again after only a few seconds. Grrrr! I really do need to sort my setting out and keep meaning to, but it always goes out of my head, so I do it now before I forget yet again. The time delay was set for ten seconds so no wonder it keeps locking itself on me, I have changed it to ten minutes now.

I click back on the fish icon and I find myself smiling as I open the first message and it starts with well hello beautiful.

I reply with a Good afternoon before opening my second message which just says Hi. I'm not being rude but the profile picture of the man, has me guessing he is more my mother's age so I don't respond.

My phone beeps again and again, I open the third message. I smile again as I read what is on my screen, this man has taken the time to read my profile and comments on how, he loves walks through the woods too, and that it seems like we have a lot in common. I click on his photo to open his profile link.

Damn! This man is good looking, far too good looking for me, I tell myself. I scroll through his photos and I can feel my cheeks burning as I come across a photo of him holding a guitar with what I am guessing is a cigarette hanging from his lips. Mum walks back into the room and I can't help but show her the photos of this dashing young man.

I am guessing he is about my age and I really like that, he plays the guitar. I have never dated anyone who can play an instrument before and even though I have always been too shy to play my own guitar in front of anyone other than my Mum or Jude, I can still imagine me having a jamming session with someone in the future, in front of an open fire would be perfect.

'Oh, he is dishy' Mum says raising her eyebrows at me.

'Have you messaged him?' she asks

'Not yet but I will do'

I decide to open a few more messages before I respond to message number three. As I open more messages I can see that most them are a little crude, so I scroll right past them. The rest are just short but sweet hello's which is okay, but when I have someone clearly wanting a conversation with me, a simple hello isn't quite good enough.

'Mum I have had over twenty messages in less than five minutes' I am amused at how much attention I am getting already.

'Told you Ella. You are good looking'

I feel a little knot in my stomach. Hearing my mum say something flattering to me is rare and I am starting to think moving away from everything I knew back in Manchester wasn't such a bad idea after all.

'Thank you, Mum I love you'

'I know you do' she says passing me my tea.

'Now message him back!'

'No rush Mum, it's only been five minutes'

She really is keen for me to message this man back, but I decided to look through a few more messages first. Some men really are so rude, I am being asked if I want fun tonight, and we all know what fun means.

I do like a bit of fun from time to time but I need to know the person first. I am not the type of person to have a one-night stand or fall into bed with someone just for a bit of fun. That's why I have always steered clear of these types of sites.

As if! some men really do think of us women like a piece of meat. Luckily there is a block button because I can see me using it a lot today.

I finally message back the third person who messaged me earlier, only because he seems interesting. I introduce myself and ask him how his day is going. He responses straight away which adds a little smile back onto my face.

We are typing to each other for a good few minutes when my Mum looks over to me smiling, she has been looking at me off and on and I am guessing to try and gauge my expression.

'Well?' she asks sounding almost frustrated with having to wait for me to speak.

I take a deep breath before responding to her.

'So, his name is Tylor and he is a little younger than me, but he loves museums and art galleries.'

Which sounds like an ideal date if you ask me.

'He is training to be an art teacher at the minute and he loves long walks, Mum he sounds far too good to be true'.

'Which usually means he is'

She has just crushed me in one tiny sentence.

That is another reason why I shy away from these types of sites. Men can say whatever they want, and I suppose women are just as bad. It's all about trusting that what they say is the truth, and that what they are telling you, is not some line just to get you into bed which I am sure you get a hell of a lot of, with on and off this fishy site.

I continue to message Tylor off and on throughout the evening and the more we message the more I am liking this man, he has made me smile most of the day and he hasn't really done anything special. The man is just interested in knowing more about me and finding our common grounds, he comes across as very self-assured but in a non-cocky way.

Is it bad that I have deleted most of the other messages without even reading them?

I am nowhere near as rude in real life, but I have no intention of meeting up with anyone anytime soon, and the few crude messages I received earlier has slightly put me off this dating site already.

I had to put my phone on silent before I came up to bed, it hasn't stopped beeping at me all evening and I know I should feel some form of flattery but that isn't happening at all, I feel almost tarty letting men message me all day long.

I message Tylor and tell him I am going to sleep so anyone else who decides to message can go and do one. I know that I should be happy. I am getting so much attention, but it is honestly making me feel a bit uncomfortable, but maybe that is just because I am not used to the world of online dating.

Most of the messages today were dirty men asking me to add them to Kik, so they can send me dick pic's.

Now I'm not being funny, but a man's cock only looks attractive when you know you are the one making it erect.

I am not even sure I have ever seen a photograph of a good-looking penis.

It's gone midnight and I am absolutely shattered so I am calling it a night.

I wake to the sound of my little Sister softly calling my name, she has such a cute voice anyway, but I am noticing hints of the Irish accent creeping in which make her sound adorable. As I open my eyes I see her big blues staring back at me.

'Mummy has made you coffee' she says a little too chirpy as she runs back out of the bedroom.

'Mummy she is awake' I hear her shouting as she makes her way back down the stairs a little too excited.

I reach for my phone to check on the time and I am pleasantly surprised when I see that it's gone ten in the morning. I can't remember the last time I slept in so late. After a big stretch that has my bones clicking, I reach for the dressing gown that my Mum has loaned me until I get into town and buy my own. I am twenty-nine, yet I feel more like a sixty-year-old. That bed is comfortable when you first get into it, but my back is telling me a different story now.

Mum is living room is hardwood flooring and cold under my little feet, as I found out last night, so I put on a pair of socks before making my way to the bathroom; my bladder feels tender, so my body has clearly needed the toilet for hours. After a quick wash and a scrub of my teeth, I make my way down the stairs and into the living room.

Mum's made me a coffee and rolled me a cigarette. I am very grateful and thank her as she hands me my cup.

'I am heading into town today if you want to come?' she asks.

I cannot wait to see the city and jump at the chance to be shown around. Mum offers me breakfast, but I can't eat when I have just woken up and I tell her I will treat them all to lunch in town instead.

'You really don't have to' she says in a concerned tone.

'Mum I want to, so don't argue'.

CHAPTER FOUR…

'This place looks amazing'

I am taken back as we were walking into the heart of the city centre and the tall old buildings come into my view, the architecture and detail that has gone into every building has me looking up as high as I can see, and I hadn't realised until now, just how close my Mum lived to the main city centre. When she said, we were walking it in, I was dreading the concept but now we are here I can see why she opted to walk.

'It would take longer to get a bus or taxi in, because of the traffic' She said as if she could read my thoughts.

'Has that man messaged you today?'

I had honestly forgotten to check my phone, apart from to check on the time when I first woke, so I couldn't tell her, and I hadn't changed the setting yet, so my phone is still on silent.

'I don't know' I said smiling and I can see a little frustration in her eyes.

'Why don't you look then?' she asks all curious, but I want to play on it a bit, I think my Mum is more excited by this mystery man than I am, and it is amusing to watch.

'I will when we get back home'. I smile before looking back up at the imposing old bingo hall that has taken the sun from my face, it looks like it has been derelict for years and it's a pity as the bingo hall is the only eye sore I have come across on my walk so far.

We have been in town for hours, but I still don't want to go home. I know we should though as the kids are starting to get bored of walking around the shops with us, Mum has bought them both new clothes, but I'd imagine that isn't much fun for a child and they would have much preferred money spent on toys or sweets.

I am pleased as punch with some of the bargains I have got today. Three dresses and all for under a tenner each.

I don't wear dresses much these days, but Mum talked me into getting them while they were so cheap, and you never know if I am lucky, someone will ask me out for a drink at some point soon. There is me saying I wouldn't be meeting up with a man from this dating site, but I am already hoping Tylor likes me enough to want to meet up with me for a drink.

'That green one will look stunning on you' Mum says as I removed my new clothes from the bags.

'Thank you, Mum, green normally does suit me so I hope so' My dark auburn hair and green eyes have me steering towards deeper shades lately and I think this dark forest green is my favourite colour because

I have a pair of trousers and a jumper both in the same shade.

'Go and try them on' Mum says as she makes her way into the kitchen to put her shopping away.

I squeeze myself into the green one first and I must say it really is figure hugging but covers me enough that I don't feel tarty. This dress feels great and it was only a fiver. I do love a good bargain. Call me a cheap skate if you must, but I don't think I ever really buy anything when it is full price, unless I have no other choice of course, and then I moan about it for days on end, only in my own head like, but it does frustrate me paying full price for something I might only wear once or twice.

I put my heels on and fling my hair up in a loose bun before making my way back down the stairs.

'See' Mum announces, 'You look amazing and no one would guess it was a Primark dress'.

I had to agree the dress felt quality and did have an original price tag of eighteen pounds, which is still stupidly cheap for the quality of the dress.

After trying on my other dresses and showing my Mum we, both agreed that the green one looked the nicest on me.

'You can wear that when you meet this man you have been talking to' she says all excitedly.

'That's if he even wants to meet me Mum' I raise my eyebrows at her and she laughs.

After I have left my phone for half an hour to charge I check my notifications and almost spit my tea all over myself.

'Mum I have had over one hundred messages' I shout into the kitchen.

'Any of them from the one you like?!' she shouts back at me.

'I don't know yet' but I am hoping so.

A lot of the messages are from people who I haven't replied to, some of these men are really insulted that I have seen but not replied to them and others are just plain rude.

After deleting and blocking most of the men who have tried to message me, I finally open a message from Tylor.

He has asked me how my day is going and told me that he had been out for a walk in the woods and that it would be nice if I could join him one day.

Is he asking me out on a date?

I would like the first time this man sees me; for me not to be in my worst clothes, because you cannot walk through the woods in a nice pair of shoes, my trainers are scruffy and need replacing. So, I message back and tell him that I would love to, but I think he should invite me out for a drink first.

That was brave of me, and normally I wouldn't be so forward but if I am being honest with myself. This man seems to be the only one who is keeping hold of my attention, before meeting him I have a very good feeling that we will get on well.

It is almost seven thirty in the evening when Tylor responds and asked me if I wanted to meet up in a few hours. I know I said I want him to ask me out soon, but I didn't expect him to ask me out tonight, I am not mentally prepared.

'Mum! he wants to meet me tonight' I screech.

'You best go and get ready then' again, Mum sounds more excited than me.

I'm not sure I am ready to meet with him just yet, we have only been talking for forty hours or so and to be completely honest I still have my mother's voice at the forefront of my mind. That comment she made yesterday about how people lie all the time just to get women in bed has me worried.

I am now wondering in self-doubt, but I really do hope Tylor isn't like that. I think if I found out he was; I would just delete this app straight away and forget this whole stupid online dating business. I would have to just go about dating in the traditional way, after all it seems to have worked for our grandparents.

Just the thought of me going out on a date is alien to me.

I have obviously been in relationships but all of which have been coincidental and just sort of developed into something. We would spend time with each other and just assume that we were an item, without really having the conversation. Before I have known it though, I have become bored and unhappy and after putting up with feeling this way for months, or even years I finally had enough and eventually walk away. Most men have been unfaithful in the past, thinking that just because I am laid back and come across as nice and understanding, that I would just forgive them, but I will only take so much before I say enough is enough. It takes me to feel betrayed or even threatened in some way, for my nasty side to come out but ninety percent of the time the world gets to meet the nice, polite Ella Roberts.

Even though I am apprehensive I am still getting ready to meet Tylor, this is what I was hoping for after all.

My dress is on and I have opted for the green one, I showed my Mum earlier today. I agree it looks good on me and shows off my curvy waist. I have left my hair in loose curls and just have my makeup left to do which won't take me long. I have a younger Sister who lives in Essex with our father and she has told me that it takes her nearly four hours just to apply her makeup, she goes on about how she contours her face and uses highlighter and bronzer. I wouldn't have a clue what half the things were, and I am surprised if my makeup takes me any longer than four minutes, never mind four hours. I feel like a teenage girl and it shows with my shaky hands. At this rate, I will look like a clown and be going nowhere. So, with an hour to go before my taxi, I make my way downstairs to have a much-needed smoke to calm my nerves. The last date I was on, was over three years ago and I am worried it will be written all over my face.

Jude set me up with that Darren a few months ago, but I couldn't class eating our food in silence and me escaping the restaurant as a date, can I?

Mum walks in the kitchen behind me.

'Ella, I don't think I have ever seen you act so nervous' she says with a sympathetic look on her face.

'I will be fine, after my smoke'

She looks at me and shakes her head, Mum doesn't smoke herself so has never seen the appeal. After applying my makeup and squirting my favourite perfume all over my neck, I am finally ready to go and now I am feeling nervous as hell.

'So much for that smoke calming my nerves!'

CHAPTER FIVE…

Tylor has been texting this past hour and has admitted that he doesn't normally ask someone out on a date, so is a little nervous himself. That thought should make me feel more at ease, but it doesn't, and I almost jump out of my skin when the taxi beeps outside. I message Tylor to tell him I am on my way and he responds to tell me he is already at the pub and will meet me outside.

My hands are clammy, and my mouth is as dried up as an orange skin left out in the sun for far too long.

The taxi stops outside Annie's Tavern and I can see Tylor is stood by the doorway. His one hand in his pocket and the other one smoking on a cigarette.

Fuck me, this man looks more attractive in real life and his photograph's do not do him justice.

Then there is my own photo, which makes me look a lot better than I really am. Shit! now the nerves are kicking in on overtime. I don't want to get out of this taxi, but as the driver passes me my change, I know I have no choice.

No backing out now Ella; I give myself a mental note as I open the car door and step out. I walk towards Tylor almost too shy to look up at him.

He really is devastatingly good looking with his well-maintained beard, and very green eyes. Now I wouldn't normally be attracted to a man with facial hair, but he really suits it. I'd say he has an almost nineteen twenties look to him in his flat cap and blazer combo.

Totally fuckable is my first thought and I am almost telling my brain off for being so rude. I am glad the thoughts are in my head because I have no idea if this man will find me attractive or if he will even like me.

'You must be Elouise?'

Shit that accent has me melting on the spot.

I obviously knew he would have an Irish accent what with being from Belfast and all that, but his voice is deeper and more seductive than I had imagined.

'Please, call me Ella' I say as I feel myself blushing.

'Drink?'

'Yes please' my mouths so dry that the words barely escape my lips.

We make our way up the stairs and into the bar. It has quite dull lighting, but the music has me thinking I might just like this place, it is a far cry from the pubs I am used to in Manchester and it is not as busy as I half expected it to be, but it is a Tuesday evening after all. Tylor asks me what I want to drink as we make our way over to the bar, it's an easy choice because I only ever drink rum.

'Noted for future reference' he says winking at me.

I can feel my cheeks getting warmer again, he seems just as self-assured in person as he does through text. I smile to myself as we make our way to a table, but I am still feeling a little awkward. I remove my coat and I am very grateful to be relieved of a little heat.

'It seems very warm in here' I say placing my coat on the seating beside me.

'Wow' Tylor announces on a grin.

'I like your dress.'

He flashes me a cheeky grin as he takes his seat beside me and my stupid cheeks catch fire all over again.

'Why thank you sir, you do look rather dashing yourself'

Oh my God I can't believe I said that out loud, I am feeling shy and cannot wait to get this first drink down me.

I take my drink in my hand as Tylor reaches for his own holding it out, so we can clang our glasses together.

'Here's to a good evening' he says raising a toast.

We decide to make our way outside to the smoking area and Tylor has just admitted that he was as nervous about meeting me this evening too. He said it in text earlier but hearing him say the words to me instantly makes me feel better, and before I know it, we are both talking freely, and our conversation turns to our common interests. We just seem to hit it off straight away and there are no awkward pauses. I do feel like I am talking just for the sake of it at times, it's a little nervous thing I do but Tylor seems happy enough chatting about all sorts of random topics. As the topic turns to food I confess that I am a fussy eater. Tylor says he can tell for all the size of me. He can't talk, he isn't exactly a big man and if I was to guess I'd say he was about five-foot eight. That is only eight inches taller than me.

Just the way he is speaking to me is seeming to influence my body. So, by the time the topic turns a little flirtier my mind is going on overdrive, I can't help but think about rude thoughts as we start to talk about our sexual interests and it is very clear to me that Tylor has had experience. I know with some people that might put you off but for some reason it just makes him seem a little more mysterious to me. I have only ever been with a few men, but I know I am far from inexperienced myself and I have never had any complaints in the past. Tylor seems very sure of himself which I am really starting to like. He isn't arrogant or cocky with it and tells me that it is just because he knows he is a good guy, and I have the feeling he is telling me the truth.

The night seems to evade me far too quickly and before I knew it, hours have passed.

'Do you fancy a little drive before I drop you home?' he asks.

I must have looked a little surprised.

'Just thinking we can have a cheeky smoke before I drop you off'

My first instinct is to tell him that I am okay, after all I do not know the man, but for some reason I ignore my doubts.

'That would be lovely actually' I smile as Tylor helps me with my coat.

He then takes our empty glasses back to the bar and thanks the bar staff before holding the door open for me.

'Why Thank you sir'

I feel my heart start to race again as I realise I have just agreed to go out in the dark for a drive with a man I have known for only a matter of hours. There is something about Tylor though that makes me feel at ease and I have just messaged my mother to tell her where I am heading just in case.

We start walking up the street to where Tylor has parked his car, well I say his, he has just told me that we can't smoke in the car as it belongs to his Mum and that his own car is in for repairs.

As we get towards the car Tylor opens the passenger door for me. He comes across as a gentleman and I thank him as I take my seat.

It is pitch black and the drive isn't very well lit so

I have no idea where he is taking me, but he has me feeling safe enough as he tells me more about himself and his dreams to become a full-time art teacher. It is really endearing to see someone have so much passion about something and it has made me think about what I want to do with my own life. I have always wanted to be a writer, but I don't see how I could ever make a career out of it.

Tylor insists that if you want something enough you can make it work for you, but as much as I like his outlook on life, I am nowhere near as confident about my ability as he is about his own.

We slow down, and I can see an industrial estate in front of us, now I am a little weary and ask why he would bring me here, he explains that this is the road he takes to work and points to a big building in the distance and says that I should feel sorry for him as he will be stuck in there in less than twelve hours. Just as I am about to ask why his workplace would be the ideal place to stop for a smoke and I am hit with the view of the ocean in front of us. It looks almost mesmerizing as I watch the moon reflecting off the calm waves.

'Beautiful, isn't it' Tylor says seeing the big smile on my face.

I love nature in all its shapes and forms and Belfast has some amazing views so far. We pull up by the sea front. I can tell this is a lovely spot even in the nightly glow and I can only imagine how beautiful this place would be on a warm summers day.

The sea is within touching distance and the only thing between us are some oversized boulders of blackened rock.

Once we both got out of the car I look up at the cloudless, sparkling night sky while Tylor starts to walk over to the large rocks, he climbs up making it look easy and turns back around to face me.

'You should come and stand up here' he shouts just as the wind picks up in my ears.

I just laugh and shake my head at him in disbelief.

'I can't swim Tylor, so you wouldn't catch me up there' I confessed. I think he is slightly shocked or amused.

'Honestly, you never learnt how to swim?' he asks in a slightly sarcastic tone, now I can tell he is a little amused.

I shake my head at him feeling slightly embarrassed.

'No and nor do I wish to, I had an accident as a child and it put me off for life' I explain.

I had an accident when I was ten years old that put me off the water for life. I was the new girl at school and my parents had refused to buy me the googles in needed for our swimming lessons. I was shy and didn't want to ask anyone if I could borrow a pair of googles and I had to jump into the water and retrieve a black rubber block from the bottom of the pool. It was only one and a half meters deep but as soon as the water hit my eyes, I closed them tightly. I obviously didn't see the metal steps and my head collided with them, spilling my head open. I was sent to the hospital and I remember my parents being annoyed because I had interrupted their day. I haven't been in a swimming baths since.

I don't go into detail on way I cannot swim, but it has me thinking about it.

'I love swimming, it makes you feel free, and I think it is the closest thing to flying in my book'

Tylor walks back towards me and when I look up at him I can't help but smile.

'It is beautiful here, freezing cold but very beautiful' My voice sounds shaky and I am clearly shivering.

He smiles at me, which makes me feel a little shy.

Tylor then lights up his pre-rolled cigarette and puts his arms around me using his jacket to shield me from the wind that is now picking up with some force.

I wouldn't normally like being hugged or anything, but I feel relaxed in his hold. I smile to myself as Tylor passes me the cigarette. I guessed he was going to kiss me when I felt his mouth close to my neck, but I can see that he is too much of a gentleman to do anything without checking first. It is weird, it seems like I have known this man for a while, even though we only met properly a few hours ago. I feel safe in his hold and that is something I don't think I have felt in a very long time.

I am disappointed as I feel the cold hit me as soon as he releases his hold, and I am feeling almost deflated as he starts to walk back around the car.

'I will take you home, so you can get warmed up' he says opening the passenger door for me.

As much as I am gutted that he hasn't made a move on me or anything I know that I can't let anything happen on the first night, what would the man think of me? Although if he does decide to make a move when he drops me off at my Mother, I am uncertain that I would be able to control myself. My mind is going crazy and I can imagine him ripping my clothes right here and now, I have been known to be a sexual person in the past, but this really isn't like me on a first date. I am grateful that these thoughts are in my head because I would hate to think what Tylor would think of me if he knew I was having these fantasies already. I think I would scare the poor man away.

I am frustrated and almost ache to feel his lips against mine but I'm not stupid or naïve, and ignore my urges, for now anyway. I can honestly say this is the first time I have been attracted to a man so soon, what with his good looks, those dazzling eyes and oodles of personality, I am feeling rather lucky indeed.

The drive home is quiet, so I am left to my own thoughts and half wondering what has Tylor so quiet, he has been chatting up to now, and I am starting to wonder if I have said something wrong, though I can't recall saying anything that would put him off me. Well I don't think I did.

As we arrive outside my Mum's house there is a little awkward moment as I undo my seatbelt.

I think about leaning in for a thank you kiss but am a little worried he will turn me down and I don't want to look foolish, so I just smile at him and bid him a goodnight.

I think he would have happily kissed me, but I didn't take the chance and end up going to bed kind of regretting that I didn't make my move. Hopefully I haven't scared him away though because I know I was doing nervous talking half the night.

Nervous talking isn't good either, I tend to give my whole life story and don't think before I speak, but Tylor seemed fine with me and said he would message me tomorrow, so I hope he is true to his word.

CHAPTER SIX…

I think about messaging Tylor as soon as I wake up just to tell him that I had an exceptionally good evening, but I don't want to seem too keen, so I do nothing. Well I say nothing, I obviously scrolled through his social media feeds and I am completely blown away by some of his artwork he has showcased online. I know he said he is training to become an art teacher but damn this man has some talent. I find myself daydreaming about how handsome Mr. Tylor Richards is, and cannot help but think of what he might look like under his clothes when I see a photo of him with his shirt undone.

Our conversation last night had become a lot flirtier than I was expecting, and my poor mouth is feeling it today. Between smiling all night and biting on my lower lip, it is left feeling a little tender. My mind has me thinking about how things could have turned out if I had kissed him while he had his arms around me, would he had taken things further than a kiss I wonder?

How am I even thinking this shit? Suddenly I feel like a naughty teenager and smile to myself in amusement.

It has been a while since anyone has made me smile like this, but I can't help but think that the world will implode, and all will go horribly wrong, call me paranoid but I have always seemed cursed when it comes to relationships.

Not that I am either looking nor want a relationship of any kind but after talking to Tylor I am a little unsure if I could turn down a bit of fun with this man, and from the conversation last night Tylor seems to be singing from the same hymn sheet as me. You hear it all the time lately where two people have the benefits of a relationship but without all the strings attached and that was what Tylor said he is looking for in the dating site we both use.

He admitted that he had been on a few dates, but nothing really came of them and I am hoping that won't be the same with me, but with him not kissing me last night I am finding it hard to read the situation.

By midday Tylor has messaged asking if I want to meet up with him again, I have already agreed to babysit my little brother and Sister this evening, so I ask him if he is free tomorrow.

I hope he doesn't think I am making up an excuse.

It's over an hour later before he replies, and, in that time, my stupid childish mind had started to wonder if, that was all it took for him to go off me; was one knock back enough for him to lose interest? but I was wrong, and Tylor has jumped at the chance to see me tomorrow evening instead.

My face is starting to hurt with this new smile that has taken over it and my Mum has noticed too.

'I can stay in if you have plans Ella' she says after I told her about the message.

'Do not be silly, Tylor is fine waiting till tomorrow' I say reassuringly as I can 'besides he can't have too much of a good thing, now can he?'

I feel a ping of nervous energy just at the mention of his name, what the hell is wrong with me? Clearly my hormones are screaming out for some attention.

'Well only if you're sure'

'I wouldn't say it Mum if I didn't mean it'

Thursday night has come quick enough and before I know it Tylor and myself are in a cozy pub near where he lives. The bar is very traditional with nautical paintings mounted on the wall. Old tankards of all shapes and sizes hang from big meat hooks and the space looks very warm and inviting with the dark wood cladding on the lower part of the walls. This is a perfect little pub in my eyes and I feel fully relaxed around Tylor tonight, though he seems a little off himself, I have only met him once, but he seems a lot quieter than our last date, maybe it is his turn to be nervous.

Tylor heads to the bar and ordered our drinks.

He then turns around and just smiles at me.

He has an endearing smile and I notice he does seem to smile quite a lot. I can feel my cheeks getting warmer and I think he must know I am starting to feel uncomfortable with his silent smiling, and he seems to be playing on it a bit.

Tylor returns to our table with two glasses, he has opted for a local beer and I have had my usual Jamaican rum and coke, with a hint of coffee. I like the fact that he didn't ask what I was drinking and remembered from the other night what my favorite drink is. He sits back down beside me, but this time a little closer. I can feel my heartbeat quicken as he leans in towards me and tries to say I have something in my hair. I don't think I do have anything in my hair, but I play along. He gently places his hand in my locks and his lips on my cheek. My cheek! I thought the man was going to passionately kiss me on the lips and I find myself feeling shy suddenly.

I cannot help but let out a nervous giggle.

He then kisses me on the cheek again but this time whispers in my ear and asks me if he can kiss me properly. I let out a small moan as his lips touch mine.

His kiss is soft and gentle, and I can feel the motions in my core start to erupt as our tongues meet. He is enticing my mouth open, and I am accepting him freely. I need to close my eyes and take this moment in completely. Tylor's kiss is very seductive and leaves me wanting more as his face moves away from me again.

Me being as shy as ever, I look away as the heat of him leaves my body. To be honest when I look back up at him, he looked just as flighty as me.

'I am really sorry, but I have wanted to do that since I met you' he said looking away himself, I think I have just seen a small glimpse of shyness from this very confident man, and this makes me smile to myself.

I informed him that I really don't mind, and that he should have kissed me sooner if that was the case. After that initial first kiss, our conversation turns a lot flirtier, and has trumped our first dates naughty bander, by a mile off. All this sexual talk is killing me inside.

It has been at least 18 months since I have been with anyone. Through my own choice though.

I have had offers, but I just felt like I had lost my sex drive and the thought of a one-night stand has never appealed to me. Sitting next to this beast of a man though, my body is telling me a completely different story and it is clear from our conversation that we both agree there is a strong sexual connection between us.

Tylor seems to be more relaxed around me again. His egotistical confidence is through the roof as he goes on to explain all the naughty things he has been daydreaming about earlier in the day.

Then can you believe had the balls to suggest that we both find somewhere a little more secluded, so we could give into our passions?!

I have myself been daydreaming about him off and on throughout the day, and with how aroused I am at just the thought of this man being in an embrace with me, I know that it is on the cards at some point. Without sounding like a tart, I had almost hoped tonight would be the night that he would at least make a move on me and maybe feel my leg up. I made sure my dress is a lot freer flowing this time, making it easier for it to creep up if it needs to. I have a feeling that my underwear may be a little too inviting for him to ignore, as well.

'Oh Mr. Richards you are very keen' I try and act coy.

'Can you blame me? look at you' he waves his hand and nods his head in appreciation.

As we stand up I notice his hardened manhood and I can't help but smile to myself. It is only eight in the evening and we have all night to go before I finally decide to take him up on his offer. His kiss seriously has me wanting a whole lot more. I won't try and lie and say that I don't want to have him fuck me silly right here and now on this table but just because I think up these situations doesn't mean I will act upon them. I am more worried about what Tylor might think of me if we did fuck on our second date. Why I let my mind think so much is beyond me and as it turns out, by ten o'clock I have agreed to go for a walk with him in the nearby woods.

I feel like a naughty teen; who is meeting up for a quickie in the woods, we all did it growing up I am sure, having to find somewhere just to kiss or maybe more because we still lived at home with our parents. I had one friend growing up called Emma, and her mother would let her take her boyfriend's back home overnight. Emma's Mum would say if she was having sex in her house, then at least she knew her daughter was safe. Which as an adult I can kind of see where her mother was coming from, but I couldn't imagine my Mum hearing me at it. That is like so wrong, on so many levels.

Both Tylor and myself live at home with our parents too, so, the woods seem the perfect place to give into our urges.

Tylor has suggested that we pleasure each other up against a tree or over a fallen log, but I am conscious that someone might catch us in the act and I would be mortified if I was arrested for indecent exposure. Imagine me having to explain to my Mum why I wouldn't be home that evening, I am sure she would see the funny side, but it is a chance that I am not willing to take, plus it isn't the warmest of evenings.

I feel nervous again but at the same time I kind of don't really care, my stupid nerves can just go and do one because I am so turned on right now. My mind has me needing to feel him so badly. I feel a little overdressed for a walk in the woods and keep thinking about all the worst-case scenarios that you could imagine up, in this situation, but I'm trying to tell myself that I am fine even if the nerves keep creeping in and trying to persuade me otherwise.

I might not live up to his expectations as he talks like he is very well experienced, and I am very conscious about my so-called breasts too. They look fine when I am wearing clothes, but as soon as the padded bra comes off, which it won't. They are nonexistent and pointless even owning a pair.

I have always had my hang ups but guess so do most people.

It's dark considering it is meant to be the start of summer and only just past eleven in the evening.

'We didn't anticipate the weather did we' I say shivering and hoping he was joking about fucking me against a tree.

'There is an old barn over this hill. I used to run about up here, when I was younger' he said pointing in front of us, not that I can see more than five meters in front of us, maybe he has got us lost? I am worrying a little now.

'Not romantic I know but will be warmer than out in this wind and a little more private' he pulls me closer squeezing my cold bum.

That nervous giggle again!

'Sounds like a plan batman'.

'No' Tylor almost snaps at me.

'Just no, batman, really, what are you five years old?' he asks me like he is expecting an answer.

I'm unsure whether I have just been told off or if he is playing with me, so I just laugh it off and continued walking beside him. I can see the barn in front of us now, but it looks like it will collapse at any point. It seems a lot smaller than Tylor explained but he did say that he hasn't been up this way in a very long time, so I can't say anything to him.

As we get closer to the door which is blocked with rubble and two big planks of wood, Tylor tells me to be careful and uses his foot to move the wooden planks to one side. He then uses his foot to move some of the rubble until he can open the door.

'After you Madame'

Even though it is dark outside, the moon is shining through the windows, giving me enough light to notice a wooden bench and coffee table in the corner of this barn; which is no bigger than your standard large garden shed.

I make my way over and within seconds Tylor has joined me. We both sit down on the cold wooden bench which feels a little damp, but I am already seated and not planning on getting up again for a while.

Can he tell I am a little nervous?

I guess so as he asked if I feel comfortable enough with him, so that we can explore our urges together.

I want to rip his clothes off and give into my passion in a heartbeat, but I am nervous, and I can't hide it, no matter how hard I try. Tylor makes us a smoke to try and calm my nerves and I am very grateful to him. He really does seem like a genuinely nice person, but I can't help but feel on edge as this is so out of character for me.

'I would normally wait a lot longer before allowing a man to get so close, but there is something about you, Tylor, I'm not quite sure what it is yet' and I am being honest I say as he passes me a smoke on his cigarette.

I need him to just kiss me before I choke on the cheesiest line to date.

'There is something about you too' he replies before leaning in to kiss me.

Is this man in my head?

I place the palm of my hand on his face as he kisses me with a little more force. Then he just stops suddenly, and looks directly in my eyes, his hand cupping my face.

'Sorry' he says apologetically.

'I couldn't resist anymore, and like I said, I have wanted to kiss you properly all night'.

It is dark, but I can see his eyes clearly, melting into my very being. I don't know what to say so I just smile and kiss him again. A shiver runs directly down my spine as he moves his hand towards my jaw and starts to kiss me with so much passion and vigor. I have never been kissed like this before and I am starting to wonder; if this is how he kisses me then I cannot wait till he is doing a whole lot more to me. Tylor takes in a deep breath and I am grateful to catch some much-needed air myself.

Fuck me this man is kinky. His kiss alone is making my inside walls contract with each sweep of his tongue against mine.

We are just looking at each other for a few moments when I try to pull his body closer to mine, not wanting to feel any space between us and feeling exposed because my dress, has now creeped half way up my thighs.

Tylor's sees me trying to cover myself a little, but his hand starts to slowly make its way up to my inner thigh. Tenderly he starts to massage my leg and slowly lifts my dress even higher to reveal my new black stockings.

'Oh my' he says surprised.

'I am liking these very much so' he looks at me and smiles, as I lift my head, he leans back in to kiss me again.

His hand starts to make its way up higher as he caresses me. Inching it higher, until he finally reaches the outline of my underwear. I raise my body; teasing him to touch me some more.

As his fingers run across the seam of my knickers, I raise my hips again. My body is becoming more conscious of the attention he is giving me, and I am feeling slight tingles all down my legs.

My breath quickens its pace, as does my heartbeat and the hairs on the back of my neck have stood on end as I feel a wave of almost electrical energy surge down my spine, making me feel powerless in his touch.

I must let out a tiny whimper as Tylor looks back at me.

'Do you like that?' he asks even though it is clear to see that I do.

'Very much so' I say biting on my bottom lip a little harder than anticipated.

This man's touch is like a roaring fire heating up my body from the inside out. Tylor moves his fingers inside my underwear. The feeling of his flesh against mine is too much to ignore as I let out a long-winded moan. Any nerves I felt a few moments ago have dispersed into a cloud of erotic intentions. I look at Tylor and can see that his trousers are getting tighter as his manhood starts to harden inside them.

This stinky old barn could be a five-star hotel for all I care. What Tylor is doing to me feels amazing as he sends a satisfying tingle all over my body.

This man has very talented and creative fingers.

My body rises so he can place his fingers inside me; I need to feel him inside me before I start to explode.

Oh fuck! I seem tight as he slipped just one finger inside me at first, but he is doing an awesome job at teasing my opening with the end of his thumb at the same time.

I haven't felt this alive in a long time and really don't want to orgasm too quick and ruin this moment.

I start to undo his trousers, Tylor lets out a small moan as I run my fingertips over the seam of his zip. His trousers are getting uncomfortably tight, so I pull down his zip to finally reveal his hardened manhood. I had wondered what it might look like, and I am pleasantly surprised that he seems in very good shape and well sized. Now I know, size doesn't always matter, but I look up and see him looking at me intently, watching my every expression. I just smile back at him, nervous that he could read my thoughts.

'I think this needs to come off' he said interrupting our gaze.

He starts tugging slightly on my dress with his free hand while his other hand is still teasing me. My breathing starts to quicken again as Tylor rubs me harder and harder.

He seems to enjoy rubbing me and I have no complaints when he does it so bloody well.

'I can't take my dress off, if you are still teasing me' I look at him as he smirks back at me.

'Yes, you can, and you will'.

I just look up at him, slightly shocked by his tone, but at the same time, I think am liking this domineering side to him.

'Is it like that then?' I ask, and there's that nervous giggle of mine again.

Tylor doesn't say anything he just carries on teasing me while rubbing his own manhood. I pull my dress up over my head, knowing what I have on underneath. My new black corset is my favorite. What I love the most is the emerald green trim which matches my knickers and of course the stockings Tylor has already managed to set his eyes on.

'Wow' he says smiling at me, with that half grin of his that he does so well 'I really wasn't expecting this to be on underneath, do you know how much you get my blood pumping?'

'I have an idea' I reply nodding towards his unyielding steel rod, which is now in my hands.

I slowly rub him up and down and squeeze my grip every now and again from the pleasure I am receiving myself.

'These need to come off too' Tylor is pointing to my underwear. He has moved them to the side to get at me better but now he wants them off. He tone is demanding and strong. I do as I am asked or told, whatever way you look at it and remove my knickers. I place them on the floor by my feet hoping I can find them easy enough later.

I then shuffled back on the seat.

'No, I want you to turn around' I looked up at him and I am starting to wonder if I like his demanding tone or not, he is turning me on like crazy with his voice, but I wonder how far he will go.

I know I am overthinking and should just enjoy this moment, but I also don't want this man to think he has no boundaries with me. He must have read my face and guessed I was a little shocked.

'Please' he says, 'It's for your own benefit I promise you'

So, I listen and precision myself on all fours in front of him. I am feeling a little uncomfortable with my arse up in the air as it is and then Tylor stands back and stares at me, only adding to my awkwardness.

It may be dark outside, but that moonlight is giving us enough light to appreciate each other's bodies.

'Please sit down' I ask before getting up and standing in front of him.

Tylor looks up at me, I can see the cogs working their way around his mind. He then pulls me closer placing his hand back between my legs and proceeds to place his fingers inside me. I can feel myself tighten around his fingers each time he pushed them in, each thrust harder than the last. Feeling my body gripping him is making me wonder how on earth his hard cock is going to fit inside me. I can just about get my hands around the base of his shaft although I know that I do have very small hands, I still worry if his manhood will hurt me.

I turn around to kiss Tylor on his lips, but I don't stay long before moving down to the nape his neck. I can feel his pulse quicken and hear his breathing getting deeper. It is clear this is one of his spots, but I still asked if he is enjoying it. He nods his head while letting out a small moan.

'I wonder if you will like this' I say placing my head lower down his body.

He started to undo his shirt as my lips make their way down his chest. I am trying to be as gentle as I can, and I can see that it is making his breathing heavier. It is having the desired effect I think proudly to myself.

My lips finally touched the end of his penis, it twitches, so I gently touched it again with the tip of my nose and again his body responds in the same way. I like this effect I am having on him. I continue to gently run the tip of my nose up and down his solid hard shaft, making his erection pulsate uncontrollably. I start to kiss the end of him while running my tongue up and down the entire length of his erection. I am loving this control and I know his is going to thoroughly enjoy me sucking him off. I place my lips around him and slowly lower myself. It is a little struggle at first while I train my mouth to open wider than it is used to, but I manage to get at least half way down his seven-inch penis.

I look up at Tylor and smile.

'Fuck me Ella, that feels amazing' he says in between the subtle moans of enjoyment.

I just smile at him again and tell him that.

'I aim to please'

Tylor's legs started to tighten as I get a little deeper.

I have clenched my mouth making it feel tighter around him and then every now and again I release him for a moment and enjoy licking him, up and down and gently kissing every inch of his manhood.

I could worship this cock so easily.

I let out a moan as he places his hands inside my hair, his grip increases with my speed.

I can tell he is having trouble controlling himself but that doesn't stop me.

I am guessing if I really wanted to, I could make him explode, but I am not ready for him to finish just yet. I want this moment to last for as long as physically possible.

The feelings he is stirring inside me are powerful, and somewhat intense but I want more.

He is looking at me, his breathing erratic as he attempts to speak, his words struggling to form a full sentence.

'You, you look so fucking sexy with my cock in your mouth'

I can just about make out his words and nodded my appreciation of the compliment I have just received.

I can tell I am getting turned on by sucking on him and I can feel myself getting damp. I run my fingertips over my lips, parting them slightly as I do so.

Tylor must notice because he looks at me with a look I can only describe as disbelief. I feel his question without any words escaping his lips and I acknowledge him only by placing my now dripping wet fingers inside my mouth. Licking away my essence, his cock is still firmly by my opened, as he is twitching while watching me lick my fingers completely clean.

'You are something else' he smiles and tilts his head back, his eyes firmly closed now.

I let out my own moan of pleasure as he circles his hips wanting to be inside me again. I need to stop sucking his him because I am not ready to him to ejaculate. Not yet anyway. I smile at him as his eyes meet mine again and I lift myself to my feet. I perch my bum beside him and can't help myself when I start to run my hands over his fully erected pleasure pole.

'I don't think so, my turn' he says in a domineering tone again. I am certain I like this tone now as I feel my inside tighten and I feel the tingles in my core.

'Lie down' so I do as I am told.

'Yes sir' I reply more sarcastically than I had originally intended.

I am lay down on my back; as Tylor starts to kiss my face, he then looks at me and even though he is almost in the shadows, I can see that adorable grin spread across his face, before he slowly moves his lips towards my neck and bites down gently on my shoulder.

He can kiss my neck all night long if he wants to.

I place my arms on his shoulder teasing his head lower, and it works. I feel my body start to tingle as he finds the spot just behind my ear, that almost sends me over the edge.

This is so fucking intense!

Tylor makes his way down my body slowly but with pure intent. I let my feelings of desire come to the surface, pushing past any insecurities and allowing my hands to explore the top of his arms.

'Think you should take this off too' he has got to be kidding me, no way that is happening as he starts to tug on my bra. That's it, my walls are up again.

'No, I told you, you won't get me fully naked, I hate my body' I'm shaking my head at him and this is something he will not try and control.

'I will get you naked, I can promise you that, and I like your body Ella' he winks at me and all I can do was smile back at him.

I don't want this to ruin the moment and I'm pleased when he doesn't try and push me further.

'Mind if I explore it some more?' he asked flashing his tongue at me.

'Be my guest' Oh, my I have been thinking about this all evening.

As soon as his tongue touches me I feel my legs begin to tremble from the million little nerve endings in my body. He has an electric sensation taking over my whole body as he takes his time to tease me.

Fuck me he is good!

My poor clitoris is already feeling sensitive from his earlier attention, but I still raise my body, so he can place his fingers inside me.

'Spread your legs for me' he asks, his voice rugged and rough.

My hips start to sway in motion with him forcing his finger deeper inside me. I look down and I can see him concentrating while nibbling on his bottom lip. His eyes are languidly travelling from the apex of my thighs, up to my face.

'Do you want more?' he asks, what a stupid question really.

My panting has increased and I so, want more.

I want to feel him inside me as deep as physically possible.

This man really is opening my eyes and not just my sex. Until this point I thought I had a healthy sex life and I am taken to my own little world as he starts to pound his fingers in me harder and with more speed and vigor.

The slight burning sensation is adding to the pleasure and I can't get enough. My back arches up as he slows down his pace, slowly fucking me while he continues to flick his tongue wildly over me one moment, and then sucking me into his mouth the next, building me into a total frenzy of wanting more.

My thighs tighten shamelessly around his head as I lose myself in this state of euphoria that I had only ever imagined in my wildest of fantasies.

I feel like I am about to erupt, and I think he can tell as he looks at me with that cheeky grin again and starts licking and sucking on me a little harder, his fingers still firmly fucking me hard. Tylor quickened his pace.

Tylor carries on with force even though my nails are cutting into his shoulders, this man is relentless and doesn't give up.

'Don't stop' I pant as my body shakes uncontrollably.

I try to move away to give my breathing a second to catch up, but Tylor just follows me almost like he is attached to my groin. He stops and looks up at me trying to wiggle free, the man looks somewhat offended that I have tried to move from his grasp.

'You are not getting away that easily' he places his hands on my hips and buries his tongue inside me as deep as he can.

I'm shaking even more now, and I can hardly breath while my heart feels like it is about to jump out of my chest.

I can't take anymore.

I can feel his free hand run its way underneath me as I am lifted off the seat. I cannot take this no more and finally let myself go.

I can't remember anyone ever making me release like this before, this is crazy, and I feel like I have been in some naughty pornographic movie or something. My body is in pure bliss. Tylor is looking at me with a massive look of satisfaction which only has me feeling a little shy. Shy that I have been so forward with him already, and shy at the mess we have just made on the floor.

'Fuck me' I say panting, 'I have never cum like this before, you are good Tylor, you are very good indeed'

I'm sure he is loving being told how awesome he is, but he is, and he has just blown my mind as well as my body.

I feel like an awkward teenager who has lost her virginity or something. I have always enjoyed sex, but Mr. Tylor Richards may become my new addiction if tonight is anything to go by.

Tylor wipes his face with his dripping wet hand and looks at me. He leans down towards me, so I lift my head to kiss his wet lips. I can taste myself all over him.

'Now I am going to fuck you hard if you don't mind' He says getting onto his knees and placing my body in line with his own.

I have no energy to even try and stop him as he slowly teases me with the end of his manhood.

Sliding it ever so gently inside me and frustratingly pulling his body away again. Tylor places his hands on my hips and holds me in his desired place. My body is still in ecstasy as he slides himself inside.

He fills every part of me as I feel my inner wall grasp at him, making my sensations increase with each trust. Our bodies crashing off each other as I feel him pushing deeper and harder with every muscle in my body tensing, as his body collides with mine.

I am about to cum again!

Not that I think it is even possible considering the mess I have already made. Tylor then places his hand in front of us, I can feel his chest against my back as he starts to rub my core again. I can tell it is a little awkward for him, so I move his very talented hand replacing it with my own. He grips hold of my waist and I can tell already that this makes him crazy.

Knowing that I am helping myself reach climax again must be causing a stir in Tylor too, as he starts fucking me as hard as he can manage.

He breath quickens, and he moans out, I can tell he is about to release and I let out a moan of my own.

His grip on my hips gets stronger and I feel his nails dig into my skin, as he finally lets his fluids mix with mine.

The warm sensation of his creamy essence warming my core from the inside out.

'Wow' I confess.

'I am not finished with you yet'

This man has just finished himself inside me and he wants to carry on, wow he is a beast and I am liking it very much so.

'Come here' he says holding onto his cock that is still somehow fully erect.

'Your turn'.

I don't think I have any energy left as my legs are as stable as jelly on a plate. I try to climb over to him without looking like a complete fool but that isn't easy in this small, cramped space.

Beats being out in the cold though.

I saddle my legs over him and take his hardness out of his hands and line him up with my body, slowly teasing myself with the end of him and the gradually lowering myself down onto his full length.

Tylor is looking directly in the eyes, as he starts to grind his body towards mine, rubbing against every sensitive area I have.

I can't get enough of this man. I don't think I have ever had an orgasm last so long, but I spoke too soon, and Tylor forces me all the way down on him, feeling the head of his manhood push itself as deep as possible has my juices trickling all down his balls. Tylor is kissing my neck passionately while I notice his hand creep up to my bra strap. He tries to undo my strap, but I move his hand out of the way and I am pleased when he wraps both arms around me and starts kissing me even more.

Just then some light shines straight through the window.

I panic and quickly move, covering myself up with my dress. Mr. 'Confident' Tylor stayed where he is and doesn't seem to be fazed at all.

Tylor is laughing as he watches me rush to cover myself back up.

'I thought that was the local authorities or something' I explain as I start to put my dress back on.

'Aww you're getting dressed already, I hadn't finished with you yet' he says disappointedly with those stupid puppy dog eyes.

The face he is pulling is cute but if he thinks I am going to fuck him again while people are clearly walking about outside then he is mistaken.

'Sorry, passion killer, but I would like to continue this another time, real soon' I say trying to find my knickers in the dark.

Tylor passes me my underwear, which were clearly under his foot and has a glance at his watch.

'I don't want to kind of have my way with you, and then say right good night, I'm away' he sighs 'but it is getting late and I do have an early start in the morning' he sounds all disheartened.

'I really enjoyed myself tonight, and I really enjoy your company Ella' he gets up to his feet and makes the few steps over towards me, placing both his hands on my shoulders.

'I really do want to see you again'

'And me, I mean I would like to see you too' I blush 'we will see each other again soon I promise' I say slightly worried that this might be our one and only goodbye.

'Of course, we will, and I guarantee to get you naked next time' he says confidently with that cheeky laugh and extenuating the word will.

'If you say so' I am shaking my head at him because I know it won't happen.

I warned him on our first date that no man has ever seen me naked and that's how it stays. Plenty have tried in the past but ultimately have given up arguing with me.

'I do Ella, and you will learn, I am never wrong'.

He seems so arrogant at times, but I think I like it.

CHAPTER SEVEN…

Mum wants to know everything about last night, but I feel a little ashamed of myself. I have known this man for less than a week and he has already got me in bed. Well a small cramped, disused barn but you know what I mean. I have been known to be reckless in the past but not with my own body. I just couldn't help myself.

'Well how did it go?' she asked passing me my morning coffee.

'Good' was all I managed to say but she keeps looking at me expecting more.

'Mum, I have done something stupid' I finally confess.

I went on to tell her about our evening, obviously missing out the in-depth detail of our erotic encounter but still admitted that I had slept with him.

'And your point is?' she asks.

I was half expecting to get the third degree off her but instead she goes on to tell me how I have nothing to be ashamed of and that I am young, free and single. She tells me it is my life to do with as I please and that I haven't hurt anyone, so I shouldn't feel ashamed in any way, and she's right.

Last night was the most fun I have had in a long time and I am now wondering why I feel so dirty.

'Mum you know I never give in so easily'

'Well you must really like him Ella'

'I think I do'

It's just past two in the afternoon and Tylor has messaged me to tell me how he has been thinking about me all morning. I am so glad he can't see my face because I have suddenly got really embarrassed. The message went on to say how he hopes to see me again.

I smile and send my reply.

I really enjoyed myself too and looking forward to seeing you again soon x

I wasn't going to add a kiss at the end of the message but after running over the message a few times I felt it needed it. I just hope he doesn't read into it too much.

He replies within minutes asking if I am free this Saturday afternoon. After checking with my Mum on whether she had made plans for us, I reply telling that I can't wait to see him.

I am in town and it seems busy today.

I can feel myself getting flustered as I try to remember the mental shopping list my Mum gave me before I left but I cannot concentrate for the life of me.

What the fuck is wrong with me?

I have had sex once and my hormones are going crazy turning my head to mush and all I can think about is last night. My body experienced something it really isn't used to and now it is screaming out at me and begging me for more. I have heard of women being turned on just at the thought of sex but had never really grasped the concept until today. I could never have imagined this is what they meant. Tylor has got inside my head and I am not sure I am liking it. I think I should head to the café for a much-needed coffee and cigarette while I sort this stupid mind of mine out.

It seems to be working for a whole five minutes until my phone starts beeping. I am hoping it is Tylor and I am frustrated when I see it is just a reminder from the dating site telling me I have unseen messages.

I haven't been back on the site since I first started talking to Tylor, so I decide I may as well delete it.

I am scrolling through and see that it hasn't got a deactivate button so all I can do is delete the app from my phone, it isn't ideal, but I feel better already.

'Hey Mum' I say all chirpy as I walk through the front door.

'You seem better now, did that trip to town clear your head as planned?' she asks.

'Yes, very much so' I smile 'I deleted that dating app earlier'

Mum looks a little shocked and asks me why, so I told her now that I have Tylor's Facebook and his phone number, I have no need to go onto the site.

'But you don't know how things will go with you and the art teacher'

She has a point, but I am not the type of person who lets more than one man give me attention, even if it is just through words. I am sometimes too loyal for my own good and have given people more chances than they have deserved. To find that loyalty back is very rare, and I am far from naive enough to think that I will be treated with the same respect. I do know that being cheated on isn't very nice and I know first-hand the hurt it causes, I have been on the receiving end a few times so, I always vowed to be as loyal as I can no matter what and that includes talking to another man, when I am enjoying Tylor's company so much.

Mum and the kids have gone out for the evening, so I have planned to have a long soak in the bath and catch up on some reading. I am reading a book about a girl who heads off to New York in search of getting noticed.

She is a singer songwriter but hasn't had much luck in England, so she heads of in search for a better life.

I can relate to this book a little as I have not long moved away to start a new life of my own. My bath is ready, so I make my way upstairs but stop in my tracks as my phone starts ringing. It is charging in the kitchen.

I half sprint into the kitchen almost slipping into the worktop because my socks hold no friction on the tiled floor.

'Well hello beautiful' Tylor's voice is deep and sexy.

'Tylor, how are you?' I ask.

'Very good thank you' I can tell he is smiling, I don't know how but I can.

'So, Ella' he starts 'I did have plans tonight, but they have fallen through. Are you busy?' he asks.

I inform him that I have the house to myself for the evening and that I am about to get into the bath.

'Oh, I would love a bath right about now' he sounds a little envious.

'I was thinking if you have no plans after your bath I could pop round for a cup of tea and a smoke'

'yeah, okay. Why not' I say trying not to seem too keen, but I am really pleased at the thought of seeing him again so soon. As soon as I hang up the phone I dart up the stairs as quick as my little feet will take me.

Within half an hour, Tylor pulls up outside.

I have had my bath and put a little bit of natural make up on, but I am in my comfortable bottoms and a baggy top. The man has seen me twice now all dolled up, so it can't hurt for him to see me in what I would class as my normal clothes. Plus, my thought process is; if he sees me at my worst and still wants to stick around, then all is good.

He taps the door gently and when I open it I can see he looks a little on edge. Maybe, Mr. Confident is a little shy this evening, or me being in casual clothes has put him off guard. I jester for him to come in and I am a little surprised when he leans down to kiss me.

His lips are as soft as ever and I can taste his minty breath as he places his tongue against mine.

'Good evening' he then says removing his flat cap and starting to undo the buttons on his coat.

'Coffee?' I ask.

'Tea please'

'Sugar?' I ask making my way into the kitchen.

'Two please' his voice has followed me, so I can tell he is standing behind me at the kitchen door.

I flick the kettle on and I start to feel the hairs on the back of my neck stand on end as he presses his body against my back, pushing me forward slightly into the breakfast bar. He then pushes the kettle which is still boiling towards the back of the counter.

As he leans into me, I feel his erection pushing into my lower back. Tylor lowers his head and starts to move my hair from my neck with his hand. His touch is gentle and sends a shiver down the centre of my back. I am shaking like a leaf on the inside, but somehow remain calm under his touch. I feel his warm breath against my skin, his breathing increasing against my ear lobe.

'Do you see what you do to me?' he asks.

I know I can't speak, I am too captured in this moment, so I just give him a small nod of my head and let out a small moan.

'I have been struggling with this all day, thinking about you' he confesses.

I turn to try and kiss him, but instead he takes a step back from me. My body is immediately noticing his warmth evading me and all I want to do is feel him against me again. I take a step forward only for him to take another step back.

'You promised me tea' he says smirking at me, my face must be showing my frustration.

'You Mr. Richards are a tease'

Feeling slightly frustrated and totally turned on already I make my way over to the fridge. Tylor is leaning up against it and not looking like he is going to move out of my way.

'I can't make your tea, without milk' I point out the obvious.

He kisses me on the forehead before opening the fridge and passing me the milk. After adding the milk, I pass it back to him and notice him rummaging inside the fridge.

'Are you hungry?' I ask.

'No, I am just a noisy bastard who loves looking through other people's things' he smiles at me closing the fridge door.

'Be warned, I am yet to go through your underwear drawer' I almost choke on thin air and I am hoping he isn't being serious.

'Maybe when I have my own place, but everything you see in this house belongs to my Mum. I have a guitar and that's about it'

Apart from my underwear drawer that is, and a few items of clothing piled on a chair in my Sister's bedroom.

'I think I would like to see this guitar' he smiles at me before talking the cup that is starting to burn my hand off.

'Be careful it's hot' I warn.

'I would expect it to be, I just seen you boil the kettle'

Oh, he is a funny fucker isn't he, though I notice he is making me smile cause my cheeks are starting to hurt already. I don't think I have ever met anyone quite as blatantly cheeky and sarcastic. I leave Tylor in the living room while I go to fetch my guitar from the bedroom. It probably needs tuned in because I haven't played since I got here, and the unfortunate thing probably got bashed about on the plane.

When I return to the room, Tylor has made himself comfortable on the sofa. He looks at me and flashes me a big smile.

'It needs tuned in' I say passing him my old faithful.

I am pleasantly surprised when I go to pass him the tuner and he informs me he doesn't need it. Tylor has finished tuning in the guitar and starts to tell me that he has been back to the barn this morning and goes on to say that we have somehow broken the floor in our sensual embrace. My stomach almost turns as he tell me how the smell of sex still lingered in the air.

'I did warn you my bum is big; no wonder we broke the floor' I smirked at him.

'No, it was rotting away to nothing, at least we gave it a good send-off' he joked 'but I do like your big bum, very much so' He makes his way back towards me and sits down on the sofa beside me.

'Oh, do you now' I smile 'I like that you like my bum'

'Yes Ella, I really do, and that outfit you had on the other night has been on my mind ever since' he says with his crooked half smile.

'You, Tylor make me want to do all sorts of naughty things'

I think I have grown a pair balls overnight, this man brings out my mischievous side and with that this new-found confidence. Is it bad that all I want to do is jump on top of him?

Tylor starts to pick the guitar. I can play but I have never been able to finger pick, and I tend to strum the song instead. I am wishing I had two guitars now, because I think it would sound lovely with our different playing techniques. He only has the guitar in his hand for a few minutes, before he places it against the wall beside us.

'That can wait for another time' he smiles at me and taps his knee.

I place my leg over his and sit on him so that we are facing each other. I am gently kissing his neck; his hands start to rub on the top of my thighs.

'I think you should show me these naughty things Ella' he whispers in my ear while squeezing his grip on my legs.

Tylor's hand then makes it way up my leg until he reaches the rim of my baggy trousers. Slowly he moves them to one side, gripping them away from my body. He places his free hand inside, cupping my groin.

'I, I in-ten-end too' I try to speak just as his fingers cross the outline of my underwear.

'Sorry what did you say?' he asks pushing his fingers harder against me.

'Never mind' I bury my head into his neck.

I can feel my breathing is clearly getting deeper.

I raise my body towards him as he tries to place his finger inside my knickers and at first, I don't stop him, but I want to have my fun first. I hold his hand to stop him, and he looks at me with a confused expression. All I can do is smile back at him as I raise my body giving us a little space between us.

Tylor is biting down on his bottom lip as I start undoing his trousers. He is fully aroused too, I remove him from his boxers. Smiling to myself as I do so.

He seems to like me taking control a little.

I placed my hand around his erection, moving it up and down slowly and intently. I can tell he likes the way the palm of my hand brushes over the end of him.

I then lean down towards Tylor and using the very tip of my tongue I gently lick his neck. I can feel his heartbeat against my lips as I slowly start kissing behind his ear. Tylor arches his neck giving me more room to devour him, but I am conscious about hurting him or biting down too rough.

'Don't mark me' his voice is stern.

I didn't intend to but now that he has said it, I am left wondering if it is because he doesn't want anyone to know about me. Maybe Tylor has a wife that I don't know about but rather than question him and possibly make a bigger deal than is needed, I decide to stay quiet. After all I don't want to ruin this moment and put the thought to the back of my mind.

'May I suck your cock?' I whisper in his ear instead.

'Oh fuck, yes' he says seeming almost desperate to get his trousers and boxers out of the way.

I lift myself, giving him a little more space and while doing so, I remove my own trousers. I place myself back onto his knee. Tylor starts to nibble on my bra, I can't feel it though through the padding and tell him as much, he just smiles at me.

'I wouldn't know you keep them well hidden'

'And that is how they will stay' I say lifting my body from his.

I climb down so I am on my knees in front of him and start to lick the end of his manhood, it starts twitching which makes me smile. I do like how easy I seem to find this spot of his and making his manhood flinch near my lips is teasing me as much as I guess it is teasing him.

Tylor is looking down at me with a massive grin across his face. So, I place my lips around him keeping our eye contact. He makes a gasping sound as I ever so slowly take him deep, inside my warm, watering mouth. I am enjoying the feeling of him inside me, rubbing off the roof of my mouth, his skin is soft against my tongue.

He still hasn't taken his eyes off me, so I start to lick the entire length of him, slightly brushing against his balls with the tip of my tongue. He flinches and moans but the look in his eyes has me a little unsure if he likes this or not. For now, I will leave his balls alone, but I have a feeling he will enjoy it.

Tylor then starts to lift my top, trying to get it above my head so I help him, throwing it on the sofa beside him. I am sat in my comfortable black knickers, a plain black bra and my thick fluffy socks. Tylor then has the cheek to try and undo my bra. I lean back to stop him, looking him straight in the eyes.

'Told you Tylor, I won't take my bra off' I sound offended and I kind of am.

I am grateful when he doesn't push the matter and

I continue to suck on him, I think I am enjoying this more than usual because of how turned on I am around him. The man doesn't have to do much to raise my body temperature and send my pulse racing.

I can tell he is enjoying me teasing him and I am guessing the urge is getting too much for him as he places his hands within my long hair, wrapping the length of it around his palm, that increases his grip. He then places his other hand on my head and gently starts to push it down, allowing him to evade deeper inside my mouth. I gag slightly but then soon take control again.

Getting deeper and faster while my tongue massages the side of his penis. He suddenly releases my hair and I feel his hands move to my shoulders.

'Stop' he says panting.

'What, was it too much for you?' I ask as I stand up and wipe my mouth dry.

Tylor laughed, shaking his head slightly.

'No, not at all, I just really need to taste you' he says pointing to the sofa beside him.

Really, all I want to do is carry on sucking him, but I suppose I best let him have his fun too.

He stands up in front of me, cock in hand and starts playing with himself so, I lean forward to touch him, but I am rewarded with a slap on the hand.

'Did I say your allowed to touch me Miss Roberts' he says all assertive.

He tone is sexy, and my body is liking the way that he says my name.

'I didn't know I needed to ask' I am holding onto my now, stinging fingers.

'Tonight, you need to ask' he says in the same tone, that half smile appearing over that fucking beautiful face of his.

I lay back down on the sofa with my feet on the floor and my legs ever so slightly apart. Tylor kneels on the floor and starts to remove my bottoms and underwear. He looks at me for a while before he starts teasing me with his thumb, rubbing on my hood in a circular motion.

The pressure inside me is increasing with each lap.

Tylor then directed my hand and placed it where his thumb had just been.

Clearly, he wants me to tease myself and I am fine with that. Well that is until he stands back and watches me, now I feel a little uncomfortable.

I do like the way he is looking at me though. His stare is captivating, drawing me in closer to him.

I gently place two fingers inside my core and notice that I feel very tight this evening so, I raise my legs higher, making it easier to invade my insides. The sound of me getting wetter is clearly doing things to Tylor as he starts to tug at himself in front of me. This only adds to my own enjoyment as my fingers pound inside me with force. Tylor lets out a moan and I notice him slow himself down, I am guessing he isn't ready to end this just yet. I remove my fingers and place them in my mouth, more so because I know how crazy it made him the other day. He smiles at me while I am looking directly in to his eyes, my fingers still in my mouth. I can tell how much this is teasing him and it is proven when Tylor kneels before me and starts to gently lick me. My leg flinches as he moves his tongue, slowly back and forth. I need to see him, so I lift my head.

Oh God, he is really getting into this.

I can feel myself tighten as he places his fingers inside me. I am conscious that my moans are getting louder with each thrust of his hand and it seems that it is making him push even deeper. He is fucking me hard and fast with his fingers and I can feel my opening stretch around him. It stings a little, but I don't want him to stop.

'Harder' I beg in between moans. What am I fucking crazy, it sticks but I find myself begging for more.

I can feel the pressure building up inside me.

My body arches and tightens as my orgasm takes hold of me. I know I am moaning loudly and I am sure the neighbors can hear me, but I don't care. This is intense as I feel a gush of orgasmic energy rush through me and I feel my juices force their way out of me and all over the sofa and floor.

Shit! I must clean it before Mum gets home tomorrow, but right now I couldn't care less.

Then Tylor lets my body relax as he removes his fingers and starts to kiss my stomach. I feel myself slump onto the sofa, finding just as much strength I need to catch my own breath, though I have a feeling he isn't finished with me yet with the look of intent in his eyes. I am really starting to like this look of his. The man makes me feel sexy and it has been a long time since anyone, even myself, has made me feel this way. I start to blush as he leans down to kiss me on my forehead.

'Think you need to turn the cushion over' he says as he tugs my jellified legs to one side, so he can sit beside me. He has just sat in the wet patch, but he doesn't seem to care one bit. I just looked up at him and smile. I can't find the words.

'I think it is clear to say you enjoyed that' he says trying to catch his own breath. I just smile at him and nod my head.

'Give me a second and I am going to fuck the life out of you' he sounds very confident.

'Promises, promises' I manage to say as he pulls me closer and hugs me. I am lay on his chest with his arm around me and resting on my waist. I am so content in this moment and could happily fall asleep.

'Come here' he says pointing to his hardened manhood.

'Sit on me, I want to feel you stretch around me'

My legs are still like jelly but seeing him holding onto himself has me wanting even more.

'Oh, is it like that again' I am biting on my lower lip.

I stand up and saddled my legs either side of his waist and I place my hand around his full length. I use it to rub against my clitoris for a few moments before lowering my body on to him. I am aware that seem looser now due to him stretching me and the fact that he has just made me cum so much, so I tuck my belly in, to try and force my inside walls together, not that I think it works, but I try it anyway.

'I am still soaking wet' I feel like I need to say something as I am sure Tylor has clearly noticed.

'I know, it's great, isn't it?' he tightens his grip on my hips.

Our bodies move in sync with each other, grinding as he invades me deeper, and harder. He then forces me to slow down, his hold on my hips, pulling me towards him in a slow sensual motion.

'Stand up, bend over and spread your legs' he snaps in that demanding tone again, so I do as I am told, the smile on my face is hurting my cheeks.

Tylor makes his way around me and seems to be admiring my big arse. I feel the sting as his hand collides with my cheek. He automatically apologies and says that he couldn't resist.

'Gently' I say holding onto the stinging area.

'No, I told you I was going to fuck the life out of you' he is smiling at me but sounds very serious.

'Now bend down and expose yourself for me'.

I think it is best I do as he says.

Tylor is stood behind me and pushes himself inside me with ease. I take a deep breath in and hold in my stomach again. My body tightens around him, making Tylor pick up pace. He lets go of my hip on the one side and artfully unclips my bra, making it fall to the floor.

He is fucking me so hard that my stomach is starting to hurt a little, but I try to ignore the pain. I am bent over with my hands on my knees and even though Tylor is fucking me hard. Deeper than I think I have ever been fucked before, this feels sensual, and somewhat special. Just then my whole body tightens, and I can feel myself release. Tylor grips my shoulders and pushes himself deeper, only adding to the sensation of my orgasm.

I move my hand up in between our legs, going straight past my opening and start to massage Tylor's balls. His legs start to tighten and his breathing increases, so I know he is enjoying what I am doing to him.

I guess he is almost ready to explode so of course I carry on massaging him but this time with a little more pressure. I run my hand slightly lower to find the spot between his balls, and butt hole.

The area is easy to find, and Tylor has spread his legs, so I can get at him better, so, I apply a small amount of pressure again. He is loving this, and I feel like a right tart, but I can't help it, and cannot get enough of him.

He really does bring out the inner kinky bitch in me, and I feel no shame in it whatsoever.

Tylor grips hold of my shoulders, pulling me up towards him just as he lets out a big long moan.

He has finally let himself go deep inside me, his hands still firmly on my shoulders, as I feel him warm me up from the inside out.

I feel stupidly uncomfortable as he tries to place his hands on my chest. I brush them away, but he just makes his way back towards them. Again, I push his hands away, but he just slaps my hand and then whispers in my ear that I have nothing to be ashamed about.

Easy for you to say Mr. Confident. You're not the one standing here with your chest exposed. I hate not having a bra on, my breasts are nonexistent, and being so small may make me look athletic, but I feel vulnerable under his touch. Eventually I give in and let him slowly tease my nipples with his fingertips. I lay my head back, so it is resting on his chest as Tylor kisses the sensitive area under my ear lobe. I still feel uncomfortable and hate my tiny breasts, but I would be lying if I said that this didn't feel nice. Tylor must feel my awkwardness and turns me around to face him. He kisses me and pulls me closer to him, our naked bodies crash against each other, as he holds me in his embrace. I am loving the fact that even though he has this control streak which I think I like, Tylor remains the complete gentleman, and I can tell already that he is someone I can trust completely.

With my chest, firmly against his, I place my arms around him. Tylor is breathing in deeply so, I start to run my fingertips up and down his back in circular motions, he arches slightly as my finger reach his waist line.

'I could have you doing that all evening' he confesses.

I am sure he could, but he has just fucked every ounce of strength I have. I breath in his beautiful earthy smell and smile to myself as I lay my head on his chest.

'I need to stop soon' I say after a few moments 'My arms are achy'.

Tylor pulls his puppy dog eyes at me again.

'Please don't stop' he says pushing out his bottom lip and looking like a sulky child.

That is an adorable look and I can imagine it has got him out of so much trouble in the past, but I am telling myself that it isn't going to work today. My arms are starting to feel heavy. but that look does it for me whether I want to admit it or not, and I don't want to let him down by saying no. So, I agree to another few minutes.

A good few minutes have past, and I am starting to feel cold now as well as achy. For a second there, I had almost forgotten that I am stood here naked and I am not impressed. He did warn me that he would succeed in taking my bra off, and had I not been off in my own orgasmic dimension somewhere I am sure I'd have stopped him. As soon as he releases his hold of me I start to miss his heat again. Is that stupid? I have never missed anyone's heat before. I look up at him and give him my best sulky face, but he just laughs at me and tells me that it won't work on him. I walk over and reach for my bra which is lay on the floor by the kitchen door.

'I am not impressed' I say.

He must have kicked it away when it fell earlier.

I am startled when I hear him speak from behind me.

'Did I say you can get dressed?' he asks.

'No but Tylor I told you I feel uncomfortable.'

'Do I make you feel uncomfortable?' he asks walking towards me.

I freeze on the spot. I don't know why I freeze but my body and brain are refusing to engage. Tylor doesn't make me feel uncomfortable at all. Being naked is at fault here.

'No, you make me far from uncomfortable, but I did warn you what I am like' I say trying to defend myself in some way.

'Then what is your problem?'

I look down at myself and then back up at his sparkling green eyes. For the first time in my life I am feeling rather foolish for covering myself up. I still do though.

Tylor takes my bra from my hand, throwing it back on the floor and leads me to the middle of the room.

'I don't see what your problem is, you have a very sexy body' he says

Yeah right. I know I am not ugly, and I am grateful that I am naturally thin. I can get away with eating anything I like and never put much weight on but being slim isn't all it's cracked up to be, especially when one is as flat chested as me. I cannot believe he has won! I am annoyed that he said he would do get me naked and achieved that.

Oh, god what's he doing now?

My eyes are covered with what I am guessing is my little brothers school tie. Tylor must have seen it on the other sofa when he first walked in.

'Do you trust me?' he whispers as everything gets dark and I am blindfolded.

'Of course, I do' the words escape my mouth so quietly, I can just about hear them myself.

'I will never hurt you Ella, I promise you'

I can feel he has moved away from me, but I don't know where he is. I try to listen to hear his breathing.

'You trust me, don't you?' he repeats his question only worded different.

'Yes, Tylor I trust you' my words are clearer, and I can feel him close to me again.

Strangely enough I have only known this man for a week, but I do trust him wholeheartedly. I barely know anything about him, but I can tell he isn't going to do anything to put me in harm's way and that's all I need to know for now. I feel his hand on my wrist as he starts to raise my arms above my head.

'Hold them there please' he says softly into my covered-up ear. I nod so he knows I understand him.

'You're a doing as you are told, that's good' he says I can hear a small giggle leave his lips.

I can feel myself blush and I am very conscious that my small breast must look even smaller with my arms stretched up high. Tylor runs his fingers across my nipple. It tickles.

'Stay still' he says a little more demanding this time.

I didn't realise I even moved but clearly, I have.

He runs his finger over my other nipple.

This time I force my body to stay completely still. I want to put my arms down. They are already sore from running my fingers up and down his back as it is, without being in this distress position as well.

'Can I put my arms down' I ask.

I then feel Tylor's fingertips run from my wrists down.

I flinch everywhere as his fingers encounter my arm pit. I am so ticklish there and he is using it against me.

Before I know it, we are rolling around on the floor, my eyes are still covered but my arms are now wrapped around his neck. He is kissing me. I can feel the magical explosions happening in my brain again but this time it is more intense.

The lack of vision has me deeper in this kiss than I have ever been before, and I can't get enough of him.

Tylor loosens the blind fold and his beautiful face comes into my vision. He is so good looking it is unfair. I smile at him as he pulls me closer, I think he is about to kiss me again but instead he places his head on mine and holds me close.

'Thank you for trusting me' he says.

He has no need to thank me at all. I trust him because he hasn't given me a reason not to yet. That might seem a little foolish, he could be a serial killer for all I know but I highly doubt it. We must have been laying here for over an hour now and we are still both very much naked when Tylor announces that he best be making tracks as he has work in the morning. I look up at the clock and I am surprised when it is nearly quarter to two in the morning. I know Tylor starts work at eight and feel a little guilty for keeping him out so late.

We both start getting dressed again and Tylor gives me a long kiss just as he picks up his coat.

'I will see you soon' he says before kissing my forehead.

'Told you I would get you naked next time'.

He seems very proud of himself.

CHAPTER EIGHT…

I cannot sleep for the life of me.

It's almost five in the morning and I feel drained.

I have already been up and down the stairs twice washing the sofa cushion and then again to put it in the dryer.

Oh, my fucking God he was relentless again tonight.

I can't help but smile a stupid big grin and roll back over onto my side. I swear I can still smell him and I know I need a bath, but it can wait till I wake up. I want to enjoy this moment for as long as I can.

My alarm is going off, means it is nine and my Mum is due back just after ten, so I know I need to get up and tidy up. I really don't want to and huff and puff in annoyance. I throw the covers off myself before flumping up to the most arched sitting position you can imagine and then placing my head in my hands. Why did I have to have such a shit night sleep.

Tylor had fucked the life out of me and I should have been exhausted and slept like a baby.

Next time he should fuck my brains out and maybe I'd get some sleep. Sorry I can't help but smile at that thought.

That bath was so needed, my body is just tired and not as achy now. I can hear Mum downstairs, so I finish drying my hair as quickly as I can.

'You washed the cushions for me' she says as I walk into the kitchen.

Very observant of you mother.

I'm not thinking it is wise to tell her the real reason that they needed washed, so I tell a little white lie and say I split my coffee over it when I was half asleep.

She believes me and would probably die on the spot if she found out the truth.

After I make her a coffee we sit in the living room and I ask how her night away was. She had visited an old friend from school. Now had she asked me to have the kids I would have assumed that she was off on a naughty weekend with one of the mystery men she is always talking to, but she did take the kids, so I believe her when she starts talking about her old friend Karen.

I still give her my most, I don't believe a word you say look, but she just laughs it off and tells me that if she has a date, I will be the first one to know.

'Anyway, enough about my love life, what about yours?'

What can I say? I can't exactly tell her that I sneaked him in last night and he spent hours pleasing me into oblivion. Or can I? I flash her a big grin. No, I know she wouldn't see the funny side to it, so I just casually inform her that I have planned to see him Wednesday evening.

Tylor had already told me he is out with his friends tonight and has a family thing to attend to on Tuesday, so he has asked to see me the day after.

'You seem to like him'

'I do, he seems really nice from what I know of him so far' I tell her.

Though nice isn't a word I would use for Mr. Tylor Richard's. I can think of plenty and as much as he seems like a nice person, it is not a word I would normally use.

Maybe a little self-assured, totally and utterly hot and a complete gentleman. And fuckable beyond belief.

Even when he is being a total control freak he has been gentle with me and has asked before doing anything. Well apart from the blindfold. Although I am glad he didn't ask because I might have said no and ended up regretting not feeling the senses I felt last night.

'Ella' I hear Mum saying my name.

'You look like you were in a world of your own'

'I'm just tired Mum, I didn't sleep very well last night'

'Well go and get an hour's sleep while the house is quiet' she says pointing to the stairs.

I am not going to argue with her and would really appreciate a sleep right about now, even if it is just half an hour or so.

'Goodnight, morning, whatever you want to call it' I say getting to my feet and blowing her a kiss.

'I will wake you in a bit love'

'Thanks Mum'

I wake up just after three in the afternoon, My Mum has left me sleeping most of the day, but I must have needed it though, so I really can't complain. Tylor messaged me just over an hour ago, clearly, I was dead to the world because normally my phone would wake me up. I open the message.

Hey Ella, I don't have to do that family thing tomorrow night, if you don't have plans already I was hoping I could take you out for something to eat :)

I reply telling him that it sounds like a great idea.

Then receive a message asking what I am doing. I think twice about telling him I am just getting out of bed, but I send the reply anyway.

Did I really fuck all the energy out of you last night Lol :p

Yes, Tylor you most certainly did x

His response has me blushing as he sends a big reply.

He tells me the things he wants to do to me when he next gets his hands on me.

How the fuck can just his words alone influence me?

My poor lady bits contract as I read the words in front of me. As much as I am tempted to relieve myself of all this sexual tension, I am reminded I am in my little Sister's bedroom and stop myself.

Oh, Tylor you wait till I get my own place.

CHAPTER NINE…

I have been seeing Tylor now for just over three weeks and everything is going brilliantly though I am starting to worry I am falling for this man already. Which should be a good thing, but I can tell it's not. Tylor and I have both said we don't want anything serious, yet already I am gaining stupid feelings for him. Speaking to Mum doesn't help either, she says I need to tell him how I feel but that isn't going to happen any time soon.

He is due round later and I just know I am not in the best frame of mind at the minute. Here's hoping after this flat viewing I feel better otherwise I may have to cancel on him and Tylor has told me that he doesn't deal with rejection all too well.

'Mum hurry up' I shout into the hall.

I would have viewed this place on my own had I known she would take so long to get ready. I really want this flat, but the landlord was very cagy on the phone and said he has people viewing all afternoon.

Finally, she is ready, and we head out the door.

Luckily the place I am viewing is only a few minutes away, but I had planned to get there early, now it looks like I will just get there on time.

The outside looks massive.

It's an old Victorian town house

'I am guessing it is only the bottom half' I say to Mum looking up at the three-storey building.

Mum is too busy looking down at her phone and doesn't acknowledge what I have said.

A few minutes waiting when a blue BMW pulls up outside the building and a small grey-haired man appears from the driver's seat. He looks down at the folder in his hands and back up to me and my Mum.

'Which one of you is Elouise?' he asks quiet abruptly.

I lift my hand as he walks over to shake it.

'Andrew' he announces before walking towards the door of the property.

'Pleased to meet you' I reply, but the frosty reception has me wondering otherwise.

We follow Andrew inside and I am taken back a bit by the vast space of the hallway, tall high vaulted ceilings, has me feeling very tiny in here indeed.

'Wow' Mum gasps as we walk into the living room, again the space is impressive, and the tall open fire place is striking with its dark wooden surround and marble hearth. I make my way over to it admiring the wood with my finger-tips.

'It is the same height as me' I say pleasantly surprised.

Andrew then leads us into the main bedroom, this room is just as big, and I can really see myself here already.

I smile at my mother and she gives me a small half a smile back, before we are led into the bathroom.

This room looks like it could do with a little tender loving care, but with a large corner bath and two main windows and can already picture it the way I would like it.

I am a little disappointed when we are led down three steps towards the kitchen. The kitchen seems tiny in comparison to the rest of the building and the cupboards have easily seen better days but again I can see the potential. After talking with Andrew, he asks me if I am interested, and I am.

Back at my Mum's house I can't stop talking about the flat we just viewed, and Mum agreed with me about how ideal the place is, location wise and the size of the flat but with others looking at the property I am half expecting not to receive a phone call back.

'He has a lot of others viewing the flat today, so I highly doubt I will get it' I say voicing my concerns to my Mother.

'Don't be silly' she states, 'all landlords say that just to get you to panic into agreeing'

'Yeah I guess you are right' I say feeling a little deflated.

I needn't have worried though because just after an hour of being back at my Mum's I have a phone call back offering the tenancy and it is arranged that I meet Andrew back at the flat the next day to pay the fees and sign for the flat.

I am so happy that I message Tylor and let him know. It is over two hours later when I get a response from him.

So happy for you x

For Tylor that response is very short and sweet, I hope he is okay.

Just think of all the things we can do in my own place :) x

Oh, I know.

Either he is busy, or he just cannot be bothered with me at the minute, but either way he has my mind going into overdrive. Tylor is so attentive and wouldn't normally send me just small, straight to the point messages.

It's almost six in the evening and he has planned to come and see me in two and a half hours. I make my way up to the bathroom to get freshened up and apply my makeup, but I feel a little sick. Something feels off, but I can't quite put my finger on it.

I should be happy that I have my own place now, but until I have them keys in my hand I won't let myself get too excited. Mum has noticed I am feeling pretty-low too.

'What is up with your face?' she asks

'I don't know' I say, and I honestly don't.

'I thought you would have been over the moon that you have that flat'

'I haven't got it yet' I respond, brushing my hair in the mirror while looking at her in the reflection.

'Oh, Ella' she sighs 'you are not your normal self today'

I know she is right but I'm okay.

I am just not as enthusiastic as normal, but I am okay.

'I will be fine later' I say looking at the clock.

Tylor is due in half an hour, but he hasn't text me since this afternoon, so I am hoping he still turns up.

It's coming up to nine and I still haven't heard from him, so I send a message asking if we are still meeting up. I have purposely messaged him on Facebook, so I can see when he reads the message. He gets it straight away, but it is another ten minutes before he replies telling me he is sorry, and can we do something tomorrow instead.

I'm more pissed off than anything now.

Not that he is busy but that he didn't bother saying anything earlier. I have been getting ready and waiting around for hours and if he knew he couldn't see me then he could have as least said something when I messaged him about the flat. Although with the mood I am in, I am starting to think it is probably for the best.

Mum is doing my head in a bit now too, it isn't her fault, but she is questioning what Tylor could be up to and I really don't like the ideas she is coming off with.

She is right though as much as I wish she wasn't.

Tylor and I haven't spoken about seeing each other exclusively so the man could quite easily be out with another woman tonight instead of seeing me.

I am hoping not but that thought is with me all evening and still on my mind as I head up to bed, it is just after midnight and I have planned to be up early. I message Tylor to say goodnight and force myself to stay awake hoping for his reply, but it doesn't come, and I finally drift off to sleep.

I am awake early and the first thing I do is check my phone. Tylor didn't message me, but I was hoping he had while I was sleeping.

Why the fuck am I getting so annoyed?

Now I am pissed off with myself for feeling so needy and starting to wonder what I have got myself into.

Last thing I want is to fall for anyone, but I can feel me falling hard and fast and I am starting to I think I need to put a stop to this before I end up getting hurt.

I have gone through the best part of the day in my own little daze and before I know it, it is five o'clock and I am meeting back up with Andrew to sign my tenancy.

It was a lot quicker than I expected, the man seemed to be in a rush so once the cash is handed over and I have signed the paperwork, the keys are placed in my hand and he has left again. Leaving me alone in this large flat to ponder over the prospect of finally having my own space again. Now don't get me wrong it has been nice having the company of my family, but I have been in Belfast for weeks now and looking forward to the peace and quiet that comes with living on your own.

I message Mum to tell her I have my keys and even she says that it was quicker than she had guessed too.

Now I just need to get furniture to fill this huge space, but I know my Mum has been online sourcing second hand stuff for me, so I am not at all worried.

My only exception being a brand-new bed. The thought of being in a bed and sharing a stranger has slept in or even had sexual intercourse in, just turns my stomach a little. Although it is almost six so the shop I was intending on visiting is about to close. Sure, it will still be there in the morning, but I know what I am like. Once I have a plan in my mind, I expect it all to come together quicker than usually possible. I wouldn't say I am impatient but just very eager to get things done in record time.

Tylor is ringing me.

For a second, I don't want to answer the phone, but I know he hasn't done anything wrong, so I answer it anyway.

'Hello beautiful, how is things' he asks.

I tell him that I am good and that I am in my new flat.

'You don't waste any time, do you?' I can tell he is smiling down the phone.

'I like to get things sorted quickly' I explain.

'I can tell' he laughs a little laugh and then asks, 'Are you free later?'

I am free but after he stood me up last night part of me wants to tell him I have plans but at the same time I have missed him and can't wait to see him.

'I will be about eight if that works for you' I try and sound coy, but it doesn't work.

'Fancy meeting for a drink after eight then?'

'Sounds lovely Tylor, see you then'

'Will you be at yours or your old dears?'

'My Mum's house' I say, 'I have my keys, but this place is an empty shell at the minute'

'Won't take long to get all your stuff together'

I know it won't, and I agree with him.

We say our goodbyes and I start to head back to my Mum's to start getting ready. My mood has improved already, and it doesn't go unnoticed when I get back to my mother's house either.

'You seem in better form now' Mum says as I walk into the kitchen, placing my new set of house keys on the counter. She must have noticed the big smile on my face.

'I am, but not got time to chat, Tylor will be here in a bit'

'Oh, fair enough, are you two off out?' she asks.

'Yes, he is picking me up at eight'

'Are you going to admit to him how you feel?' she won't let this be.

'No mother, I have only been seeing him a matter of weeks. Don't want to scare the poor man off now do I?'

I smile at her as she shakes her head.

'You won't know if he feels the same if you don't speak to him'

'I know he doesn't so let's just leave it at that, plus I don't know how I feel myself, the man makes me feel completely confused' I let out a small nervous giggle as I walk out of the kitchen.

I head to the bathroom to get washed and changed. Least I don't need to shave again as I did it all last night before being stood up. I am still a little irritated, but I don't have a leg to stand on and I know it, I honestly feel like a stupid teenager.

CHAPTER TEN…

Tylor seems off with me tonight, he isn't his normal happy self but when I asked him what was wrong he just shrugged me off and pulls me in for a hug. So, I rest my head on his chest while he runs his fingers through my hair. The silence is broken when he finally asks about my own place.

'So, when you hoping to move in?'

'I have my keys now but don't have anything in the house yet' I explain.

'Fancy showing me?' he says with a smile.

Maybe that's what's wrong with him, maybe he just wants me all to himself, so I agree. Tylor releases his hold, so I can grab my shoes. I could have stayed in his strong arms for hours, but my mother's hallway isn't the nicest spot to spend the evening. I smile at myself while placing my shoes on.

'It's only a few minutes away' I explain.

'Perfect'

I am still taken back when I see the large bay window and imposing door and as we make my way up the few steps to the doorway. I notice Tylor looking up and admiring the big building too.

'It's only the down stairs' I say as I open the door.

'After you' he gestures with his hand.

I walk into the large living area and stand by the fire place.

'That's almost as tall as you' he says on a laugh.

'Well that's not hard is it Tylor'

The joy of only being five-foot; means that most things in life are as tall as me.

'It is lovely though, and I can see you sat in here in the evening with that fire roaring'

I agree and being back here makes me impatient and want to move in straight away. We make our way around the rest of the flat and as I walk towards the bedroom, Tylor grabs me and pushes my back against the wall.

His lips meet mine in an erotic embrace and for a second, I am completely in awe of him, that is until he steps back again, and I can feel his body release its hold on me. I don't like this feeling and grab him by his collar to pull him closer to me again.

'Don't stretch out my top!' he snaps.

'Oh, sorry for wanting you to kiss me again' I am annoyed he has just spoken to me like that.

'Next time ask me' he says before kissing me again.

I didn't realise I needed permission to kiss him but looks like I do. He is totally out of character this evening and I can't put my finger on it and my thoughts are justified when he announces that he is heading home and might not see me for a few days.

'Is everything okay?' I ask thinking it is something I might have said or done, even though I know I haven't given him any reason to run off.

'No, I just want to get an early night that's all, and I'm working late because I need to do some mock marking, you worry far too much' he places his lips on my cheek and makes his way towards my front door.

Tylor has teacher training every few weeks and did tell me he had training coming up, so I am guessing that is what he means by 'mock marking'.

I thought we had planned to go out for a drink or at least do something together, now I am left wondering whether he even wanted to see me, or just to see where I am going to be living. He has told me that he is possibly the nosiest person I will ever meet, but to just come around to see my flat and then leave, has annoyed me.

I don't say anything though, because after all what would I say? Anything that will come out of my mouth now will just sound needy and desperate, so I say nothing.

Tylor walks down the few steps from my front door, I see him bend down and guess he is tying his shoelace, but I am surprised when he stands back up and presents me with a German camomile flower, or a big daisy as I call them.

'I will see you Saturday beautiful'

I smile at him and he gives me his half smile back, but my gut tells me he isn't being a hundred percent honest with me. Maybe he has just had a rubbish day and that's why he is being off with me. He can talk to me and tell me whatever is on his mind, but the man has only known me a month and one thing I do know for sure about Tylor is that he is very reserved and doesn't like to talk about himself much.

As soon as I close the door behind him, I run to the bathroom. I really need to pee, and I have been holding it in since we left my Mother's house.

I place my flower on the window ledge and smile to myself, but it is almost a forced smile.

I am annoyed walking the few minutes back to my mother's house. When I return home, Mum tells me that she is surprised that I am back so early, I just tell her Tylor is busy so headed home.

'He only came to see you for an hour?' she is raising her eyebrows at me, I can tell this without even looking up at her.

'Let's hope I see him more often when I have my own place'

Mum has even said he seemed quieter than normal and I find myself defending him and explaining that he basically works two jobs, Tylor is a trainee teacher, and works a few shifts in the factory. He works all the hours under the sun, just to earn a living and pay for his studying. I think she can tell I am a little irate and doesn't push the matter.

'Your cooker and fridge are getting delivered in the morning' she reminds me.

'Oh, shit yeah, its Thursday tomorrow, I need to visit that bed place in the morning too'

I can see me being able to move in by the weekend if I can get the bed delivered before then.

'All you need now is a washing machine and a sofa and you will be able to move in' she says.

That has reminded me that I bid on a sofa last night on eBay that is due to end in the next few hours. 'I need to check my eBay'

'Bet you can't wait to have your house back to yourself' I say worried I am outstaying my welcome a little.

'Honestly love, I have enjoyed having you here and think the kids have too'

Izzy runs into the living room, she is meant to be in bed and Mum scolds her and sends her back up to her room.

'You have school in the morning and it is almost ten at night, you need to sleep' she says walking to the bottom of the stairs.

'Goodnight Ella' I hear her call down.

'Ni-night princess'

Never mind the kids but I could do with going to bed myself. I am worn out by todays adventures and Tylor has left me in a funny mood. I am not annoyed or pissed off, I just feel flat if that makes any sense and I haven't felt like this in years.

'I have won the sofa Mum' and for a lot less than I had budgeted for.

'That's brilliant and I am talking to Simon about a washing machine for you'

I have no idea who Simon is, but I thank her anyway.

Time for an early night, that's if I can sleep.

I am up early today because I have so much to do, the bed place is my first stop and Mum has agreed to come with me, so I don't get lost. Belfast isn't a big place really, but it is easy to lose yourself down all the little side streets and Mum has been over here for a few years now, so she likes to think she knows this place as well as the back of her own hand.

I message Tylor and wish him a good day before realising that I hadn't spoken to him since he left last night. He replies just as I am heading out the door, just saying thank you and wishing me the same.

On the walk into town I realise that I must be doing my Mum's head in talking about this man and I apologise but she assures me that it is nice to hear I like someone enough to talk about them as much as I do. I know I already like him too much and I think that is part of my problem.

'Have you spoken to him today?' she asks.

'Only briefly' I explain 'He is very busy with work at the minute, so I don't want to do his head in'

'I think he likes you more than he lets on'

That comment has me smiling to myself as we head down the street.

'Bus or walking?' I ask.

'Up to you, but it is only a ten-minute walk'

So, we walk into town and I notice Mum looks a little lost as she searches the sign posts pointing into the city centre.

'Thought you knew where this bed place is?' I don't mind walking around aimlessly, but I do have a lot of things to get while we are out.

'No, I know where we are going, I just haven't been down this way in a while'

Over twenty minutes later we finally arrive outside the shop and it must be my lucky day because they have a sale on. So far, this house move has cost me half of what I was expecting so I have a lovely big budget for my new mattress. I don't need a bed frame as the previous tenants had left the double bed frame in the flat, but I have seen my ideal bed so walk straight over to the four-poster. That was until I seen the price tag. It is beautiful and the carvings on the frame excel my expectations as I get closer. Someone has really spent some time and effort on the design, but I still cannot imagine anyone would pay over two-grand just for a bed frame. Well I would if I was rich, but I am far from it.

'Can I help?'

I am startled. I didn't even notice the small plump lady stood behind me.

'Just looking' I say before making my way over to the mattresses.

I can tell the woman's nose is put out of joint but with other people in the store looking around I had guessed she only spoke to me because of the bed I was looking at. I feel like I am in a scene from pretty woman, and I look down at what I am wearing. Tight black jeans and a grey baggy jumper, though I am sure I have seen famous people dress untidier than me.

Is it really that obvious that I cannot afford that stupidly priced bed?

The mattress I seen online, doesn't seem to be in stock so I ask another member of staff who seems a lot more helpful than the other woman and after a five-minute conversation I am happy enough with the price I have just paid and arrange for delivery the next morning.

'Sorted?' Mum asks as I make my way back to where she was standing.

'Yep, just need to buy bedding and that, now' I smile.

After spending the best part of the day traipsing around the shops I am beaten. Mum and I head back to my new flat to drop everything off before we need to get back for the kids returning home from school. Think a take away is in order tonight. I am very pleased with the number of things I was able to pick up for such little money, but I feel a little bad for making my Mum walk around with me for hours on end, so a take away is the least I can do.

Mum seems pleased she doesn't have to cook tonight, and Izzy and Ben will enjoy the lack of dishes.

That evening we all sit down and watch some film on the box. I am not really paying much attention as my mind is elsewhere. Thinking of Tylor again of course. I decide not to message him and to wait as see if he contacts me first.

By the time ten o clock comes around I am ready for my bed and I fall asleep almost straight away.

I am woken the next morning to the sound of my phone ringing. I jump out of bed as quickly as my brain will let me and as I retrieve the phone, the call ended.

Typical I mutter under my breath and I lay my head back down. I don't recognise the number so I after a few minutes of staring at the ceiling, I decide to go downstairs and make a coffee. I will ring the number back once I am up and awake properly.

The phone call is from the eBay member I have won the sofa off, she was lovely to me, on the phone and offered to deliver the sofas for me tomorrow morning free of charge as her husband is a van driver by trade. I told my Mother and she made a comment about me being very lucky lately. Which I must say makes a change.

I message Tylor to tell him that I will more than likely be in my own flat by the time I see him Saturday afternoon and he responded telling that it is great news and that he can't wait to get his hands on me and help christen my new pad. The grin on my face gives it away when my Mum asks if it is him I am messaging.

'Is it really that obvious?' I am slightly embarrassed by this, but unsure why.

I spend most of the day clearing out and cleaning the flat, not that it needed much cleaning to be honest. I just feel like I need to keep busy and my mattress is being delivered in less than an hour.

In the bedroom, I notice that the bed frame is uneven and as I shake it slightly it makes an awful sound. the squeaking will soon do my head in, so I head into the garden, if you can even call the small strip of gravel a garden. I find an odd bit of wood which I am guessing was from when the fence panels were replaced. This should do the trick. Back in my bedroom, I slip the wood under the shorter leg of the bed frame and again shake the frame. It still squeaks a little but nowhere near as much as it did, and I am hoping that the weight of the mattress will be enough to ease the noise. No sexy times in my bed if not because there is nothing as off putting, as a bed that makes more noise than your partner.

My flat is looking more like a lived-in space now with most of my furniture in place and a few little knickknacks dotted about that I picked up while in town.

I just need my sofa and to grab the television Mum had stored in the cupboard and I am ready to move in. I am stupidly excited, and Tylor's words are ringing in my head. I just hope he doesn't want to fuck me in the kitchen. That is probably the only room in the flat I wouldn't want to get frisky in. It seems cold and damp being at the back of the building, but I am hoping to get it sorted once I am properly in this flat.

CHAPTER ELEVEN…

Saturday seems to come around quickly, and I guess with all the running about I have been doing these past few days it has kind of taken my mind of things.

Tylor is due round in about an hour, but I decide to not doll myself up as I normally would, apart from the fact that I have left most of my make up at my Mum's house, I also don't think it is a bad idea for Tylor to see me in my comfortable clothes and messy hair again.

I am feeling a little out of sorts still and my gut instinct is telling me that something isn't quite right, and I think my paranoid head is spot on when Tylor knocks the door and seems a little quiet yet again.

I say that, but I have only known this man a while, so it could just be him, being his normal self.

I am overthinking this whole thing again, and I think that is what is doing my head in the most.

We are both sat on the sofa, with the distance between us housing the ashtray and the lighter. Tylor is making us a cigarette. The television playing quietly in the background. I have no idea what is on, and I honestly don't care. The atmosphere still seems a little tense and I know something isn't quite right, so I ask Tylor if he is okay. I really wish I hadn't of asked when he goes on to inform me that he had some potentially unwelcome news.

I sit up straight as he tells me that been offered a job in England and he is keen to take the post.

To say I am gutted is an understatement but I can't show him how much it is really affecting me, so I make my excuses and head to the bathroom.

After calming myself down and making a cup of tea for us both, I returned to the living room.

Tylor is on his phone messaging someone, but it is none of my business, so I don't say anything. I just sit back down and ask him questions about this new job offer.

We have both agreed that we will stay in touch and Tylor says he would keep in contact with me by any means possible. It is easier nowadays as everyone has phones and social media. So, feeling really deflated and now knowing why I sensed something was up, I just agree that we should chill on the sofa together. I move the ashtray to sit closer as Tylor's arm wraps around me, he kisses my head and I close my eyes, talking in his scent and trying to fight back the tears that are trying to creep their way into my eyes. He is running his fingers through my hair.

Tylor then upsets me even more when he pipes up and says that he doesn't think he will see me again, for a while at least, after this evening.

I sit up and look at him confused.

'But I thought you said that the job doesn't start for a few more weeks?' I am annoyed that he doesn't even want to spend any time with me.

I know we have only been seeing each other for just over six weeks now, but already I have feelings for this man, and starting to wonder if he ever had any feelings towards me. He sure as hell acts like he does with the way he holds me and the way he kisses me. I have Cher's Shoop, Shoop song stuck in my head now. Cher says it is all in his kiss, and if his kiss is anything to go by, you would think he at least felt something towards me.

'It doesn't but I'm going over early to get settled in, then I am taking two weeks out to have a holiday somewhere. I feel the need to relax, unwind, and have some fun before I take on this new job'.

I place my head back on his chest, feeling deflated, but I daren't show him how I really feel, and I am sure that will put him off me, even more so.

I am far from stupid and I know I don't have a leg to stand on. I would never want to ask anyone to change their plans for me, but I had been running away with the thoughts in my head and convinced myself that what we had, was something that we could build on at least.

Now I know I was wrong, naive and completely foolish.

Tylor has gone home, and I find myself sat in my bedroom, feeling sorry for myself and I think with good reason too. I thought the man really liked me but clearly, not. How did I ever let myself get so emotionally involved, when I knew deep down that it was all one sided. I am angry at myself more than anything. I think about texting him before I go to bed, but I don't.

Days have turned into weeks and I still have had no word from Tylor considering he told me we would stay in touch. Out of anger I delete his number like a dick. In all honesty, I am now in two minds to what I should be doing with my life? It is clear since moving into my own place, I am completely alone and the only time I see my Mum is if I make the effort to go and see her, which was fine to start with and with my mood so low I can't blame her for seeming to avoid me lately.

Pissed off with Tylor is an understatement but it is all my own doing. I let myself get close to him, let him undress my mind as well as my body and then I just let him walk away. The only way I can contact him now is through social media, and he hasn't been online for at least two weeks. I look at the time and notice I have literally just sat around all day mopping so I decide to have a look on Facebook again. I look on his newsfeed but kind of wish I hadn't now. It is nice to see that the man is still alive and that he has added some photo's since I last looked, but the more I am going through them the more annoyed I am getting.

He is clearly enjoying himself in the south of France, but my back is up when I see most of the photos taken, have the same woman in them. No wonder Tylor hadn't been in contact with me, his mind was clearly elsewhere.

I am raging and not because he is off having fun with a new woman but more so because I have let this man I had only known for just over a month get under my skin and he has unknowingly made me feel so worthless to him. I know he wasn't my boyfriend or anything like that, but this whole situation has made me cheapen my opinion on myself and I feel so foolish. I let this man, this almost stranger to me, get too close and I let it happen willingly. Part of me hoped that he felt the same in some way and he did an awesome job of making me feel special and making me feel like I was the only woman he was interested in, but now I just feel used and I hate that he has made me feel this way.

I know I am just overthinking as usual and I don't think I regret any of it as such, because if I had never met Tylor then I might never have understood how much I enjoy the sexual side of our friendship. He taught me things about my own body that I hadn't even imagined were possible and made me feel comfortable in my own skin, which is something that I never felt I would feel without cosmetic surgery. I would never have touched myself either in the past but lately I have started to desire those feeling again. I even invested in a vibrator when I was in town a few weeks ago, the last time I used it though was just before Tylor informed me that he was moving away.

These past few weeks I will admit that I have been thinking about using it again, but instead I find myself touching my core with my own fingertips. I try to imagine that Tylor is the one making me feel so alive while I am in this moment of euphoria.

I have found that as soon as I reach my climax I need to stop. It is frustrating to say the least. Tylor had a way of making me climax straight away and he could keep me on that level for ages.

I need to put this computer down because I am getting annoyed just seeing him. I wouldn't mind but when we first met, it was so out of character for me to be so open, why did I let this man seduce me? Well I know why. Tylor took me by surprise and I ran with it. For once in my life I was doing what felt good at the time and even though that thought scared me a little at the time. I had soon realized that it added to the rush of getting to know him even more.

Chapter twelve…

I have literally applied for every job going on the internet and apart from an interview on Friday, nothing has really come of it and I am feeling frustrated and annoyed.

This week has been bloody hard, and it didn't help when I took my frustration out on a few of the lads last night. They were kicking a ball against my wall and stupidly I opened my front door giving them a mouthful.

I really should have known that it was best to ignore them, but I didn't.

I have woken up with good intentions today but as soon as I opened the curtains I was confronted with a lovely sight. The little shits have only gone and thrown a tin of paint up against my house. Great looks like I have some cleaning to do. I change into the worst clothes that I own and make my way outside. Luckily, I manage to get most of the wet paint up by using an old pizza box. I will have to buy some paint remover during the week and sort out the rest then.

Jude must see that I am online on Facebook because she rings me. After the morning I have had, I am in two minds on whether to answer or not. We are talking for a while and she invites me back home for a while, I agree that it may be nice to have a break and then she then asks if Tylor would be joining me on my trip.

I don't want to tell Jude anything really, but she is far from stupid and I can feel myself getting upset just at the mention of his name.

'No, he won't be Jude, we have gone our separate ways' I say.

'When the hell did this happen?' she sounds shocked 'And why didn't you tell me sooner'

'Because I didn't want you to worry, sure it's nothing'

I am trying to convince myself more than Jude, but she isn't having any of it.

'Elle Roberts, I have known you most of our adult life, don't you dare try and lie to me, if it is nothing then why are you fighting back the tears?'

'I am not' I say to defend myself, but she is right, I am hurt, and I can't hide it.

'When are you, getting your silly back side over here, so I can give you a good slap?'

I laugh at her and tell her that, her comment has cheered me up.

'Good that's what friends are for'

I am so worn out today and I don't think I have had a good night's sleep in over a week and I can't just blame Mr. Tylor Richards for that. Being in this big flat all on my own has me on edge at times and if I am feeling low before bed I seem to get startled at every single noise and it takes me hours to finally fall asleep.

I make my way to the bathroom thinking if I freshen up I will feel better. Sat on the toilet with my underwear around my ankles and the toilet paper is just out of reach. For fuck sake! I mutter as I try and reach it.

It has somehow fallen on the floor and it's no good, I need to get up to reach it.

I scuffle on my feet and eventually grab it.

Fuck you Tylor!

The daisy he gave me when I showed him this flat is laying on the floor. I didn't notice it till I have just sat back on the toilet seat. You know what, I don't even want a bath now, so I flush the chain, rinse my hands under the tap and make my way back to my bedroom. The world can just do one today I am not in the mood at all.

I am only mopping about for half an hour when my doorbell goes. I think about ignoring it, but it rings again, and again.

'Okay I am coming!' I shout at the door, grabbing my dressing gown.

I didn't bother getting dressed after taking my trampy painting clothes off. I am surprised to see my mother stood at the door.

'Morning' I say as I move to let her in.

'Afternoon Ella, it is almost two'

I know what time it is, I have been looking at my clock on and off since five this morning, but I don't respond.

'You look like you need a strong coffee' she says making her way down to the kitchen.

‘Have you got anything stronger’ I joke but she just gives me the raised eyebrow look.

I used to get that look all the time growing up and I still dislike it as much today.

‘Where have you been hiding?’ she asks over the boiling kettle.

‘Here’ is all I say.

‘Oh, Elouise have you still not heard anything off him?’

‘No Mother’

I place my bum on the stool and my head in my hands, I can feel her getting close to me, as she places her hand in my hair. That just reminds me of him, so I move her hand out of the way.

‘Please don’t, you will start me off again’

She listens and continues to make the drinks.

‘Ella, I know you don’t want to hear this, but you need to snap out of it, you need to get dressed and get out of this flat’ she looks at me with a somber smile.

‘You have had me worried sick because you haven’t been around in over a week and your phone is turned off’ she continues.

‘I will be fine Mum, I just feel a little foolish’

‘He is the foolish one love, for leaving you like this’ she tries to make me feel better, but it really isn’t working.

‘If he had just stayed in touch like he said he would, then I don’t even think I would have got so annoyed about the other woman’ I place my head on the table, but I can tell she is pulling a face and I hear her gasp.

‘Another woman?’ she asks, ‘was he cheating on you?’

‘You can’t cheat on someone if they are only friends Mum’

I look at her and can still see the shock on her face.

'We were never together as such, were we?' I say reminding her of the friendship me and Tylor shared.

'Well, it looked like you were both a lot more than friends from where I was standing'

He made me feel like a lot more than 'just a friend' too.

'I know Mum, but I told you that we had a conversation about not wanting anything serious, and Tylor did admit that he wasn't the type of man to pin my hopes on'

'But you still did Ella, you still fell for him' she is right, even though I knew he would never be mine. A girl can dream.

'That was my stupidity though, not his'

Mum places my coffee in front of me and starts to roll a cigarette for us both.

'The ashtray is in the living room' I say getting to my feet to go and get it.

'We can just go in there if you want, I haven't sat on your new sofa yet'

I nod my head and she follows a few seconds later with our drinks. My Mother hadn't noticed the paint until she walked into the living room with me.

'What the hell happened?' she asks.

I explain about my run in with the lads outside and that I will need to repaint the walls and scrap the paint off once it dries on the glass.

'Oh love, that is the last thing you need' she takes a seat beside me.

'So, what are you going to do?' she asks as I pass her the ashtray.

'Well I have spoken with Jude and she has said I can go over to her for a while to sort my head out' I explain.

'And are you going?' she sounds upset.

'I think so, Belfast hasn't been what I expected so far'

'Ella, you haven't given it time love, and running away isn't the answer'

I know she is right, but running away is what I do best, even if I hate admitting, that this is what I do.

'I am not running away, I am just getting away to clear my head' I feel like I am having to defend myself a little and I am only going for a break.

'Will you be back?' her voice sound cracked as if she is about to cry.

'Yes, Mum of course, I will be back' I say this but at this moment in time I have no idea what I am doing really, I will just wing it as I usually do and hope for the best.

CHAPTER THIRTEEN…

Why I decided to get the coach and boat back home is beyond me, it would have been a lot easier to get a flight straight to Manchester airport but there's nothing I can do about it now. The coach is completely full, and I made the mistake of sitting at the back.

I have a family behind me and the small snotty ginger boy keeps kicking the back of my seat. I am tempted to say something, but I think better of it and just get out my book to read. Eventually the kid stops, and it seems like he is now taking out his boredom and frustration out on the chair beside me, but it is an older gentleman, and he soon says something to the child's mother. She tells her kid off and makes him sit on the back seat with her.

Thank God because he was really starting to grate on my nerves.

We are at the dock and I am cueing up at the security desk, my heart rate starts to increase.

I can see the passengers in front of me are having their bags checked and I remember packing my vibrator in the front zip. Why I didn't try and pack it better concealed I will never know, but it is too late to do anything about that now. I am sure they have seen it all before, but this is a private side to me, and I would I like to keep hidden. Suddenly I am washed over with embarrassment.

My bag is opened.

My perfume removed.

'I'm sorry but you can't take this' the security guard announces before placing it in a tray 'It is too big, you are only allowed 100ml'

I already knew that but didn't think about it while I was packing my stuff this morning.

My perfume can be replaced but my dignity can't as he opens the zip and starts to pull my underwear out.

I look behind me seeing a large line of people waiting to be seen, and when I look back the man is placing everything back in my bag. I am sure he must have seen my bright purple sex toy, but he didn't say anything, so I am very grateful when he passes me my bag back and wishes me a good trip.

I walk as quickly as my heart beats and I am relieved when I finally get in the cue to board the boat.

The boat sails at five o'clock but doesn't arrive in Liverpool till gone ten at night.

I then only have twenty-six minutes to get to the train station before my last train leaves but knowing my luck I will miss the bloody thing and be stranded overnight. Luckily, I do have money in my savings account that I can transfer if needed but I really don't want to do that if I can help it.

All I want to do is sleep but I wasn't going to pay the extra fifty pounds for a cabin, so I grab my big cardigan from my bag and try and get comfortable in the booth, it doesn't help that the waters are a little bit choppy and I am feeling a little sick as it is. I just hope by the time I get into my bed at Jude's house I am knackered enough that I can have a decent night's sleep.

Jude has already messaged me to say that her future husband is collecting me from Manchester train station, I am grateful because I wasn't looking forward to getting a taxi to hers after midnight. It would have cost me a small fortune.

I get to my platform with ten minutes to spare.

As I am sat there waiting, my mind is working on overdrive. I notice the train to Cardiff and my mind swims back to Tylor. I haven't looked on Facebook since the other night and I don't plan to go back on it anytime soon.

I am annoyed with myself for feeling this way, for letting him get so close and letting myself gain feelings for him, but it is done now and all I can do is try and move on and forget about him.

Once I arrive at Piccadilly station I can see Dan is waiting on the platform for me, I can see his stupid red beany hat from here. I got him it for Christmas over five years ago and he still wears it now, it needs to be binned but Jude says he isn't haven't any of it. As the train comes to a halt I let out a small sigh of relief. I decide to let some of the other passengers get off before me, just so that it is easier to grab my case.

I hate having to jump from the cart to the platform.

I am not sure why, but Manchester's tracks seem wider than most, making the gap between the platform edge and the train a good half a metre jump.

Dan has seen me straight away and makes his way over to me.

'I will take that' he says reaching for my case 'heavier than I expected' he smiles.

'I always pack too much'

'You can't be as bad as Jude, she took three cases with her when we went to visit my parents the other week'

I smile at Dan, knowing what my best friend is like.

It only takes twenty minutes to get to Jude's house and as soon as I walk through the front door Jude wraps her arms around me.

'I can't breathe' I say as she is trying to break my bones in her embrace.

She lets go of me and pats my arms. 'sorry but I have missed you'

'I have missed too Jude'.

As soon as we are in the house all the questions are flying about. Jude wants to know everything about my time in Belfast and especially wants to know more about the man I was seeing. I tried to tell her that I would talk about it all in the morning, but she isn't having any of it.

'You cannot tell me a man has made you feel amazing and tell me how perfect he seems and then when it all goes to pot just clam up Ella, that's unfair'

'Unfair' I say shocked.

'What is unfair is that I have been travelling over eight hours and I am now getting the third degree' I am smiling but being deadly serious.

'That's what friends are for, If I can't give you the third degree as you so kindly put it, then who can?'

Dan starts to giggle and looks at me.

'She has a point Ella' he butts in.

So, I start from the beginning and I can tell that Jude already likes Tylor from her responses.

'He sounds perfect' she says, 'So what happened, why did it all end?'

I go on to tell her about his teaching job in Cardiff and how he had said he would stay in touch but never did.

Jude then admitted that she has been Facebook creeping on his wall and seen that he was with someone else.

'Is she his new girlfriend?' she asks.

'I don't know Jude, he hasn't spoken to me since the day he left, so I have no idea' and I don't.

I can guess all I like, but with him not communicating with me, that's all it is; a guess.

'Well if he was as into you as he made out he was, he wouldn't have left you high and dry now would he' Dan says making his way into the kitchen.

'You are not helping Daniel!' Jude shouts into him.

'Now put the kettle on before I decide not to marry you after all'

'Yes, Mrs Marsh' he says sarcastically peering his head around the doorway.

For a second, I'd forgotten these two have planned to get married. I change the subject.

'So, have you set a date yet'

'No, not yet but will be in the summer' she says.

'This summer coming?'

'No silly, that isn't enough time to plan my big day, the summer after so about eighteen to twenty months away yet'

Jude's eyes light up just talking about her upcoming wedding and I am glad that the conversation isn't on me and my shitty love life.

By the time I get to bed its almost three in the morning and Jude has already said she wants to go into town in the morning. I just hope she doesn't expect me awake too early. Although I do have to say I have missed this bed, it is so comfortable, unlike my squeaky bed back at home.

I must have fallen asleep almost straight away because I can't remember drifting off, and I didn't even set my alarm. I can hear Jude downstairs, so I get myself up and dressed. I head into the bathroom before I make my way down the stairs. Jude is in the living room getting her daughter ready for playschool and Dan is in the kitchen. I am guessing he is on breakfast duty because the smell of bacon fills the air. For a change, I am hungry and realise that I haven't been eating properly for weeks. That isn't really anything new though and I have periods when I eat loads and then days when I can eat very little.

I know Jude won't let that slip, she already made a comment about me looking too thin, but I dismissed her.

She will notice if I don't eat properly.

Jude loves her food and can't understand anyone wanting to go on diets or give up tasty food unless it is for medical purposes only.

'Oh, your awake' she smiles at me as I enter the room.

'Very observant' I say smiling.

'I hope you are hungry' Dan says putting his head around the door frame.

'I am staved' I say, I am feeling a little sick but hoping the food will help settle my stomach.

'Are we still heading into town?' I ask but I am hoping she has changed her mind.

'Yes, I have to drop this little monster off at eleven' she kisses her little girl on the head after tying her long hair up into a high ponytail.

'We can head in for some lunch if you're up for it?' she asks.

'Sounds perfect'

I have been with Jude for just under a week now and I feel like I am out staying my welcome. I overheard Dan bitching to her the other night about how they haven't had sex in almost a week and I am wondering if it is because I am here. I wanted to say something to Jude but at the same time I didn't want her to think I was ear wigging, which of course I was.

I need some fresh air. so, I tell Jude I am off out for a walk.

'Okay but be back for five please' she says sounding a little annoyed.

'Will do'

I need to decide what I am going to do with my life, am I staying in Manchester or do I go back to Belfast? I really do not have a clue. Talking about Belfast I told my Mum that I would ring her last night and it completely slipped my mind. I grab my phone out of my bag and notice I have a message. I'm almost certain it's my Mum bitching that I didn't ring her, but my heart jumps out of my chest when I see it is Tylor. Even though I don't have his number saved into my phone I remember it straight away.

I don't want to open the text.

He hasn't bothered with me for almost a month now, so what the hell does he want now?

I am clearly still angry with him.

Seething and emotional again I make my way to the park, I haven't been here since I was a small child, but it feels like it is the best place I can escape to at the minute.

Sat on the swings; that my Mum used to push me on as a small child, I reach for my phone again and ring her.

'Ella, I was starting to think you weren't going to call me' she always seems a little dramatic, but it makes me smile.

'Sorry, it completely slipped my mind last night. How are you anyway?' I ask.

'All good sweetheart, although we are all missing you,

'When are you coming back?'

I never told anyone how long I was visiting Jude for because I had no idea myself.

'I don't know Mum' I can hear the crack in my voice.

'I am guessing you are not feeling any better?' she asks.

'I was'

'Why, what has happened?'

I tell my Mum about the text I have just received off Tylor and she of course asked what he had put. I explained that I am still too upset with him leaving the way he did, and that I haven't managed to open the message yet.

'Oh, sweetheart, you need to see what he says for your own peace of mind'

She is right, and I know I will read it, but just not yet.

After getting off the phone I realise it is almost five and I best make my way back to Jude's.

She will only get irate if I am late for her dishing up.

Jude is like me and refuses to use a microwave oven to reheat food, so if I am not back in time, she will put it in the bin. I was late on Friday and she seemed so annoyed with me most of the evening, so I do not want a repeat of that.

I get back just in time and Jude looks at her watch before throwing a dig at me about being lucky I am back.

She really needs to loosen up and let Dan fuck her or something because this mood swing of hers isn't very nice.

Not that I can talk with the mood I have been in, but I would like to think that I don't take my moods out on everyone else. Jude on the other hand doesn't care who her mood affects and has stated on quite a few occasions that she knows she can be an utter bitch but doesn't care.

Dinner is served, and we are all sat round the table in silence when Jude asks me if I am okay.

I go to say yes, as I really cannot be doing with her going on at me, but my mouth has other ideas.

'Tylor messaged me' I confess.

'The art teacher?' Dan asks and I just nod.

'Isn't that a good thing?' Jude says, 'You have been bitching that he hasn't bothered'

'I know'

'So, what has he said?' she puts her knife and fork down and looks directly at me.

'I don't know, I don't want to open the message.'

'Give me your phone here' she says placing her hand out in front of us.

'No, honestly Jude I will look later'

'No, Ella, give me your phone now'

I know I am not going to win so I place my hand in my trouser pocket and hand her my phone.

'It's locked!' she snaps before handing it back to me to unlock.

'Sorry I forgot'

I don't even want her having my phone, but I am in her house, sat around her table and eating her food. So, I feel obliged into letting her have her own way, more so, out of respect than anything else.

My heart sinks as she opens the text message and starts to read, the funny thing about it is she is trying to mimic the Irish accent, which really doesn't work.

'Maybe she should read her own message' Dan says quietly.

I bet he wishes he had kept him mouth shut, because Jude gives him her meanest glare, before clearing her throat and reading the message to me.

'I know I probably do not have the words to defend my actions, I left things badly Ella, all I can say is that I am sorry. I have been thinking about you a lot these past few weeks and I know I was selfish and possibly foolish, but at the time I felt like I needed to cut all ties to you. It was no fault of your own.

I understand if you don't want to talk to me again, but I am hoping you will forgive me in time. If given the chance I would like to make it up to you sometime soon.

Tylor x'

'What a fucking joke' Jude pipes up.

I don't know what to think.

I am angry that it has taken him this long to get in touch with me, but I can't help but smile that he finally has.

The message clearly states that he has been thinking about me.

'Please don't tell me you are thinking about responding Ella, he is a prick who clearly used you and fucked you off'

'Hey, you said you liked him'

'That was before I seen how upset you are about him, Ella you are far from stupid'

'I know I am not stupid Jude, but it is my own doing'

'See there you go again. It pisses me right off!'

'What?!' I ask annoyed at the way she is snapping at me.

'Ella, you wouldn't have said you think he really likes you too, if he wasn't showing you all of the signs. I know you and know that, this man, must have been clearly leading you on. That is why I cannot stand him'

Jude is seething, and I can tell that I should be agreeing with her, but she doesn't know Tylor like I do, and I feel the need to defend him.

'He isn't like that Jude, if you had met him yourself, you would understand' I state.

'Understand what?'

I can tell she is getting increasingly annoyed at my naivety, but she hasn't got a bloody clue, and only knows what I have told her.

'Why are you so angry?' I ask.

'Because this prick' she says holding my phone up on the opened message 'this prick hurt my best friend so much so that she came running back home'

'I didn't come running back' I put my head in my hands, I really cannot be bothered with the third degree at the minute.

'He didn't hurt me either' I defend him again.

'No, then why the fuck, are you almost crying then?'

I wish I had never mentioned the message at all, and I want to get my phone and ring him, but not while Jude is here. I know she will just shout abuse down the phone at him, and as much as I am still annoyed with him, I do not feel he deserves Jude on his warpath.

'I let myself get hurt Jude, you don't understand'

'That's bullshit, and you know it. Ella, you are like an open book and your feelings show all over your face and always have'

I know what she is saying is true, because I have always been the same. My eyes give my thoughts away and I would never have made a good liar.

'This man would have clearly seen you were getting in too deep and he still strung you along, Why, can't you see that?!' Jude is exasperated.

'I think he did. He couldn't wait to get away as quickly as possible' I place my chin resting in my hands.

'I was stupid and silly and let myself like him too much. Tylor and I had spoken and we both agreed that it was no strings, so the man couldn't have strung me along'

'I give up' Jude slides my phone across the table and gets up from her seat, almost sending it flying across the room.

'Elouise, sometimes there is no talking to you, is there?!' she shouts at me before slamming the door to the kitchen.

Me and Dan are just sat in silence.

I think I can speak for the both of us when I say that we were too scared to open our mouths straight away.

Daniel gives me a benevolent look and a half smile.

Even he doesn't see why his future wife gets so incensed about things, that don't technically affect her. After all, it is my shitty love life, not hers. I open my phone to read the message again, when I hear Dan talking quietly.

'Don't tell Jude I said this but, this Tylor dude is a man and as a man myself I know we do stupid shit all the time. He says he wants to make it up to you, which is a brave thing if you ask me and even sending that message must have taken a lot of courage on his part'

I thank Dan before removing myself from the table.

'I think I need some air'

'And I think I best go find out why she has got her knickers in such a twist' he giggles as he gets up himself, pushing the chairs back under the table.

'Enjoy your walk' he winks

'I will do, thank you Daniel'

'Remember what I said, he is just a man'

I have been out for most of the evening now. but I do enjoy a good stroll and I feel like I just need to be on my own anyway. My heads a mess and I know it.

To top it all off I am still feeling bad for leaving my Mum and friends in Belfast and being back home, or should I say Jude's. I know that this really isn't the right thing for me either and I know whole-heartedly that I have made a big mistake coming back here. With my savings slowly disappearing I know I need to make a big decision, and then there is Tylor to think about as well as all this other bullshit running through my brain, my poor achy over-used brain.

Why has he messaged me out of the blue? He left so coldly and made it clear to me that we are just two single people who were enjoying each-others company, basically I was his fuck buddy and was being used for a bit of fun.

I know I should be angry, but it was very good while it lasted, and I don't think fun is a good enough word really, but it will do for now I suppose.

I hate myself for letting my emotions control my mind. but I know it is just because I am missing him, and a lot more than I should.

Daniels words are still ringing in my mind.

'He is just a man'

It makes me smile because Tylor Richards is more than just a man.

Once I get back to Jude's, I apologized to her for walking out, but I am given a frosty response. I really wish I knew why she is getting so annoyed about all this, but I haven't got the energy tonight, so I make my way straight up to the spare room.

I reach for my phone and sit on the edge of the bed.

My hands are shaking, from a mix of being cold but also the awkward reception I got downstairs.

I open the message off Tylor again and a stupid single tear drips down my face and onto the phone screen, magnifying the word sorry.

Tylor wants to see me again, but he doesn't know I have even left Belfast, as I came back here just a few weeks after he moved himself. Or does he know? I can't see how anyone would have told him because it isn't as if either of us met each-other's friends or anything. Tylor has only met my mother because I was living with her at the time.

I set about writing a message back to him, but I keep deleting it again. In the end, I finish the message and hit send before I talk myself out of it. The message reads.

Hello Tylor… I was very surprised to see a message off you, been weeks since we last spoke.

I hope you are okay, I decided Belfast wasn't for me and made my way back home for a while, been here for a week now and already regretting it lol, How's the new job anyway? X

Tylor messages me back straight away, asking if it is okay to ring me as he needs to talk rather than text.

I am not sure I am ready to talk to him though.

What will I say? the butterflies in my stomach are making me feel light headed and sick so I decide to leave it for a few minutes before replying

I don't want to look too needy now do I?

He rings anyway, not waiting for my response.

Fuck! Now what do I do? Ignore him or answer it.

Shit! I need to get this over and done with because my nerves are shot to pieces.

His voice is a little shaky and is sounding a little nervous.

'How is my favorite lady?' he asks me.

Favorite lady is a joke, I wasn't his favorite lady while he has been off sunning himself, now was I? but I don't bite.

'Oh, I'm okay, just surprised you wanted to talk to me'

Tylor must be lost for words as the phones goes deadly quiet. I look at my screen. thinking a may have accidentally, hung up with my cheek or something. The joy of touch screen phones.

When I hear, him speak again.

'I am really gutted the way I left things and was hoping to see you Ella. I have to head home for a while' he says.

When he says home, I am guessing he means Belfast.

'I thought you were living in Wales now' I state.

'Long story but the job fell through'.

'Sorry to hear that' and I am. Tylor left everything he knew for that teaching role.

'Look Ella, I really want to see you, I have thought about you a lot, and I don't want to leave things the way they were. Will you let me see you?'

I am the one being quiet now and I don't want to see Tylor while I'm still living at Jude's. She has made it very clear that she doesn't like Tylor even though she has never met him. I explain that I am staying with a friend and that she can be funny about the thought of a man coming to her house, and that as much as I wish I could see him, I just can't. He sounds gutted but says he understands.

We both say our goodbyes and promise to keep in touch, but that is even more doubtful, now isn't it?

After the phone call, I just find myself sat on the bed, confused about what I am even thinking, never mind what I feel. I do know that I feel like shit, why was I so hasty to move back here? Have I even moved back, or do I go back to Belfast? If I go back now, then it might look like I have only moved back because he said he is, so I don't really see that I have a choice but to stay here at the minute. That sounds stupid and I know it does, after all, Belfast is a big place. If I had waited just a few more weeks, things might have been different, but I didn't and now I best just live with it.

They say everything happens for a reason and maybe we are being kept apart for a damn good reason.

I am sure it won't be long until Tylor is off again on another new adventure and I am not sure I can cope with being left behind and forgotten about again.

I know if I see him, it will no doubt all end in tears.

I won't be able to control myself, I can't control myself around him and I know, I will let myself get lost in him, I need to stop that from happening, but I am not sure I can just let him go either.

I decide to do nothing for now and just play things by ear.

It's getting late, so I turn the light off, I haven't even got the energy to get out of my clothes properly and get into bed with my trousers and t shirt still on.

This bed is so comfortable.

CHAPTER FOURTEEN…

I have been back in Manchester for a few weeks now and I have finally got my own place, it is just a rented room, but it will do for now. I can't complain either as it has its own bathroom and kitchen area so everything I need.

Even if I am still uncertain about where I should be living, at least I can call this place my own. Being back home has its benefits too and being back here with Jude is fun, when she isn't being a moody cow that is. Yet I still feel a little out of place when I am around her, being away has clearly put a strain on our friendship.

I have finished unpacking the small amount of furniture that I managed to buy cheaply from the local charity shop and after sorting it out for most of the day, I now finally have some sort of living space that I am not ashamed to show people.

Now all I need a long hot bath.

It has been a long day and I can't wait to get into a nice relaxing bubble bath, before embracing my new bed, complete with brand new bedding. To be fair everything apart from the bed base is brand new. Just as I get undressed my phone starts to ring, I would normally ignore it, but I see it is Tylor. He has been good to his word and phones or texts me daily.

'Well hello' I answer.

'Ella, I can't stop thinking about you, hope you don't mind me ringing you so late' Tylor sounds a little sleepy. I think I like his sleepy voice.

'Not at all, but I must warn you, I am naked and about to get in the bath' It is like he has a radar and can tell when I am undressed.

'Oh, now you are just teasing me' he replies with his cocky giggle.

I place my feet in the bath and swirl the water, so he can hear.

'I am so turned on right now' he whispers.

I giggle nervously 'I so wish you were here'

'Oh, if I was there, you would be begging me to slide deep inside you. Ella, I would tease you so bloody much' I can tell he is biting on his bottom lip and mimic his expression while looking at my naked body in the mirror.

'Promises, promises Mr. Richards'

'I want you to send me a photo' he sounds a little demanding which only adds to the stir inside me.

'Oh, do you now?'

I have noticed our conversation over this past week or so has been very much about what Tylor wishes to do to me when he finally gets his hands on me again.

This man turns me on like crazy and he doesn't even have to be here with me.

I am glad he can't see me right now.

I can feel my cheeks burning.

'Sorry let me rephrase that, I am telling you to send me a photo of your sexy, body please'

I burst out laughing, I try not to, but I can't help myself.

'I am really sorry, but you know I hate my body, why would I send you a photo of it?' I ask.

'Pleeeaaassee' Tylor has put on his sweetest accent possible.

'I will think about it. I don't do photos and you should know this by now' I remind him, we had similar talks last week.

'Well you should you're sexy as fuck'

I blush again and say my goodbyes.

It is almost midnight and I am lay in the bath relaxing but feeling ever so slightly aroused at the thought of Tylor and what he might be doing to me if he was in this bath with me. Just washing my body has it tingling all over and I can feel my insides tighten as I make my way up my body. My nipples are erect. I decide to stand up; making it easier to wash myself and shiver as the water trickles down my spine, heightening the pleasure I am already feeling.

I rub the soap over myself, making it form a rich, creamy lather on my stomach and I let the bubbles drape themselves lower until they reach my groin.

The sensation of the bubbles colliding with my middle has me tilting my head back and closing my eyes, the bubbles start to dissipate all over me, slowly, as I savor the moment.

I am lay back down in the bath for a while, with a massive grin plastered all over my face. Tylor really does seem to bring out my inner kink.

I decide to take a few cheeky snaps, but I am keeping them for myself for now, I haven't got the confidence to send them to Tylor and as much as I think I can trust him, I still don't want to chance them being uploaded online somewhere.

Even if I have been creative with my hair and towel so only a few parts of my body are on show, I still feel uncomfortable. While the photographs are only on my phone, I know one hundred percent, that they won't end up online. I honestly don't think Tylor would be like that, but you never know, and it is better to be safe than sorry.

Tylor and I have been in contact again for weeks now and he really does have a way with words; I receive messages telling me all the things he wants to do with me.

I am a little miffed at him though because earlier today while we were talking he did let slip that he has been with another woman that he had been eyeing up for a few days. I think for a second, he forgot he was speaking to me and not one of his friends. What am I even saying, I am one of his friends and I can't really say much because we haven't spoken about our boundaries or limits and we are both single. although knowing that he is using those talented hands on someone else does have me feeling very jealous.

I know I have no right to be and it is starting to make me wonder if seeing him again is such a clever idea.

I also made the mistake in mentioning him again to Jude who has made it very clear that she would give Tylor the back of her hand. She is still adamant that she cannot stand the man, even though she has never met him.

With the way she talks about him, I wouldn't want her to either, so I make the conscious decision not to tell her that he is visiting me at the end of the week.

The next morning, I wake up in a spin and I think I am starting to have mixed feelings about Tylor spending the weekend at mine. We are just friends, Tylor keeps reminding me of this, and we have only actually been on a few dates. I am scared because we got too close last time, or at least I know I did and that was something we both agreed that we wouldn't let happen. So, I really do have to ask myself if I really want him coming here to stay.

Jackie, who lives in the big four bedroomed-house opposite my flat, is stood in my kitchen. Cup of coffee in one hand, and her cigarette in the other. She always has a cigarette attached to her mouth, or at least it seems that way. She has popped around to bring me spare bedding and a new towel. She says she had planned to throw them away but had hoped I could make use of them.

'They are a little tatty, but would rather you use them, than me putting them in the bin' Jackie says.

'Thanks' I reply with my friendliest smile.

Jackie must have been able to tell it was forced, if I am completely honest I just want to be on my own, but I am far too nice to say that to her face.

'What is up with you today Ella?' she asks me, sounding all concerned.

'Oh, nothing really, I'm fine'

I have a lot on my mind but not really in the mood to talk about it. Jackie extinguishes her cigarette and looks back at me.

'Well you don't seem fine with me, I know when something is up your face gives it away'

I sigh and try to avoid her eye contact instead looking out of the kitchen window. Maybe I will feel better if I talk about what is bothering me.

'Do you remember the man I told you about?' I say.

'Oh, the one who had his way with you and then never spoke again?'

I turn around and want to slap this woman.

What's wrong with me? I am clearly agitated at the mention of him. What with Jude and her vicious tongue and now Jackie starting I just want to defend him.

'He wasn't like that!' I snap but I don't mean to.

'Oh, well from what Jude told me, it is exactly like that' Jackie says, reaffirming what she had just said.

'Anyway, why snap my head off, you said he hadn't bothered for months?'

Jackie speaks to Jude a lot so only knows what I have decided to tell Jude. It should piss me off that I know they both talk about me behind my back, but with Jude at least I am used to it by now. Jackie, I have only known for a few months and she really doesn't have a leg to stand on.

'He got in contact with me again, surprised Jude didn't tell you' I say feeling all good about myself for having something to throw back in her face.

I honestly just want to be on my own, and I have no doubt in my mind that Jackie will be straight on the phone with my best friend as soon as she leaves.

'Worming his way back in again is he' Jackie says looking at me again but over the top of her coffee cup.

'I knew I shouldn't have said anything' I shake my head at her.

Jackie is a good few years older than me and she is very outspoken and bold. Something that is alien to me.

She is the type of woman who would speak her mind, not caring if she insulted or offended anyone, whereas I am always told that I am too soft. That is possibly why her and Jude get on so well. They are very much cut from the same cloth.

'All I am going to say is, if you want to have fun with this guy, then go ahead but it's clear you already like him too much'

I make my way over to the tap to pour myself a glass of water, I can feel my blood boiling.

When I turn back around Jackie offers me a cigarette.

I make my way back to the table with my glass of water. My silence says it all, I go quiet when I am annoyed.

'Well you will do, what you feel is right, but don't be naive, this man is clearly using you' Jackie says clearly trying to end the topic.

Which I think is wise before it gets any more heated, than it already is. I'm not completely stupid and I know that Tylor isn't the settling down type.

Who can blame him when he can have his pick of the ladies what with his dashing good looks, exceptional manners and bags of charisma.

I think I am just grateful that he wants to share his time with me.

As soon as Jackie leaves I text Tylor and asked if he is busy.

I will always make time for you came his reply a few minutes later.

I smile, to be fair I seem to smile every time he replies to me.

I am stupidly nervous about seeing him, and if I am honest I am still a little angry with the way he ignored me while he was on his travels, but at the end of the day, I have missed him. My phone beeps again in my hand so I open the message.

I can't wait to get my hands on you, I think I will struggle to not rip your clothes off when we see each other this weekend :)

My heart starts to beat a little faster and my stupid hands have clammed up.

I am not liking this effect he has on me, which does have me wondering if I can put myself though all this again.

I am now, pacing the hallway and have no idea what to respond. Another message tone snaps me out of my thoughts.

That's if you still want me??? I really hope so x

I start to type but I have no idea what to write so I place my phone on the stairs and continue to pace.

'What do I write?!' I say out loud in frustration.

I can't tell him I am having doubts, I need time to think about this shit before I say anything back to him, so I decide to send a reply.

Of course, I still want to see you, and if you are going to rip my clothes off, I think I might just skip wearing clothes x

I leave my phone on the stairs and go into the kitchen to fetch a cloth and some cleaner, while pacing I noticed a dirty mark that is now really pissing me off.

I fucking hate feeling like this and how the fuck can one man make me feel so good about myself one minute and then make me feel cheap and worthless in the same breath.

My phone starts beeping just as I finish scrubbing the wall.

You seriously know what to say, my blood is pumping atm the text reads.

I will get it pumping next weekend Tylor x I smile to myself as I type the message.

I bet you will as well Ella ;) x

CHAPTER FIFTEEN…

This week seems to have dragged in, and I am a little nervous about seeing Tylor again, but so horny just thinking about the fun we will get up to for the whole weekend. He has been messaging me all week telling me in great-detail all the diverse ways he wants to tease me which I think has made me even more nervous about seeing him in a few days. The sexual energy between us both is electric, and I have never experienced such intense pleasures. Am I crazy to invite him here? after all he did leave and not talk to me for ages.

Am I just letting myself be used?

Maybe I am, maybe I am using him too and who says I am doing anything wrong after all we are both adults who can choose who we decide to share our time with.

Not that Jude agrees with this at all, and she has made herself very vocal over the past few days.

Jude is worried that I will start to like him too much again and is adamant that I will only get hurt all over again. I am having fun, so my best friend should be happy for me.

I decide to run a bath and get an early night, but I am hoping Tylor isn't too busy to reply to a cheeky message. I type my text and push send.

Hello, you ;) I was about to get in the bath and my mind started racing, something about being naked has me thinking about you x.

It's a few minutes later when I get a response and can't help but smile.

Hello to you too lol, you have to tell me more, I want to know how racy this mind of yours is? :) x

Do you now? xx I reply

I receive a picture message the caption reads.

Now look what you have done, no way I am going to sleep any time soon ;) x

Tylor is stood in front of a mirror, fully aroused and I am turned on instantly at the sight of him.

He then sends another message.

Can I ring you? I don't have time to reply before my phone starts to ring.

'Ah, Ella, how are we, on this fine evening?'

I can tell by his breathing that he is feeling clearly arousing himself while talking to me.

'Better for hearing your voice' I say, sounding all corny which only makes me blush.

'What are you doing?' I ask, knowing full well that he is masturbating while on the phone to me.

'Talking to you, while perving at myself'

As I close my eyes, I can picture him in front of the mirror, he is so mouth wateringly desirable. I bite down on my lip a little harder than anticipated.

'Are you still rubbing that hard penis of yours?' I ask.

'Cock, it is a cock, not a penis' he is laughing 'Penis sounds too clinical'.

'Okay, sorry are you rubbing your COCK!!' I say the last word a lot louder than needed and he just laughs at me.

'No need to shout, and yes I am, and it is all your fault, you do these things to me Elouise' I can hear his voice deepening as he lets out a small moan.

'Oh, the things I would be doing if I was with you' I say trying to hide the nervousness in my voice.

'Naughty tonight, aren't we? I hope that hand of yours is rubbing on yourself'

I start biting at my bottom lip again.

'I am soaking wet Tylor' I whisper.

'Because you're in the bath' he says all matter of a fact.

'Am I?' I ask.

I'm not in the bath yet.

'I'm going to fuck you so hard in that bathroom' he pauses. 'I want you to put your fingers inside yourself and push them deep and hard. Imagine I am sliding myself deep inside you' his voice is husky, and I think he has a very sexy phone voice.

That Irish accent really is doing the trick right now, and Tylor knows it. I place my phone on loud speaker, so I can insert two fingers inside myself.

'Oh, that feels so good' I whisper.

'No talking' Tylor says very sternly 'I want to hear you enjoying yourself'

So, I keep quiet even though all I want to do is tell him how wet the thought of him is making me and how tight my insides feel against fingers but instead I stay quiet and do as I am told.

His domineering tone has me turned on more than normal and I am sure Tylor can hear it through the phone.

I imagine him being in between my legs, licking up all my juices.

'That's it, my sexy little minx, slide another finger inside'

I am wishing I had told him now, how tight I am now.

My third finger slides inside easier than I expected, because of how wet I am.

My clit is starting to swell and is very sensitive to my touch, but I rub it anyway.

Fuck! I am going to cum soon.

'That's so fucking good' I hear him say but I still refuse to talk.

'Uh um' slips out of my mouth.

'Make yourself cum for me' he asks.

Just then I moan a little louder.

T

he man isn't even here with me, but his words take control of my body. My body which is starting to ache as I let this orgasm take over me. It is like, having him ask me to do these things to myself are heightening this feeling, I cannot control myself. I hear Tylor let out a big moan and I can tell he has also climaxed and it is confirmed with his childish giggle that follows.

'You are bad' I whisper.

'I'm bad?' Tylor's voice is slightly elevated.

'Fuck me woman, you do these naughty things to me'

'I do aim to please' I say before informing him that I need to get off and have this bath before the water cools too much.

'I made a mess' I confess in the cutest voice I can master.

'Okay then, enjoy your bath and I will see you soon' he is smiling, I can tell.

He will see me soon; the weekend is almost here.

CHAPTER SIXTEEN…

I have been awake most of the night but no matter how much I try to switch off my brain, it doesn't want to listen to me. So, I may as well get up.

I walk down the stairs holding my achy head.

It is one of these sore head where it feels like someone is squeezing the fuck out of it, like a belt tightening around your head, and it really hurts. I don't normally suffer from headaches so of course, I have no pain killers in.

Once I get to the bottom the stairs, I start to regret even getting out of bed.

'The house looks like a bomb had gone off' I say out loud in frustration.

It really isn't that bad, although, I still do not want Tylor to see it in this state.

It is just after nine in the morning when the front door goes. Who the hell is knocking my door so early on a Friday morning? As I open the front door, I am surprised to see both Jackie and Jude standing in front of me.

I can sense a telling off coming along from the scowl on my best friends' face. I can only assume that Jackie has been shit stirring.

I invited them both in, intrigued at why they are together and at my door this early in the morning.

I ushered them into the kitchen and turn the kettle on to boil.

'And what do I owe this pleasure?' I ask turning to Jude and Jackie, who are now sat at the kitchen table.

'Jackie told me, that man is coming to see you!' Jude says all aggressively.

As you can imagine it puts my back up straight away and I am annoyed that Jackie went running to Jude, but I knew she would as soon as I told her.

'Yes, he will be here, later today' I say annoyed with Jude's own tone of voice, so my reply is just as sharp.

'I cannot believe you can be so stupid and naive' Jude says shaking her head at me.

I can't believe you can be such a controlling bitch, but I leave that thought in my head.

'What time is he getting here' she asks.

'I don't know he will ring or text before he sets off.'

I sound cocky and I know I do, but I do not care.

'How do you know he will ring you first?' Jude asks me clearly getting more annoyed by the second.

'Because he needs to get my address off me' I am smiling because I have only just realized myself, that Tylor doesn't even know where I live yet.

'He doesn't know your address?' Jackie sounds a little shocked.

'Not yet, I will text him in a bit when he sets off'

'Well I think you should put him off' Jude pipes up.

'Hang on a fucking minute' I snap 'You were the one who told me to go out and find a man Jude, you never let up about it, before I moved away'

I am so annoyed now 'And now you are just completely contradicting yourself'

I do not like how this conversation is going. Jude won't let up though, and Jackie is happily adding her two pence in at any given opportunity. I am getting angrier by the second. After forty minutes of consent arguing and trying to defend myself I kindly ask my so-called friends to leave. Jackie listens to me, and sheepishly makes her way towards the exit, closing the front door behind her. She was muttering something under her breath, but I choose to ignore her. Jude refuses to leave.

'Please Jude, just go away' I say.

'No, Ella you need to grow the fuck up and stop letting this man use you' Jude stands up and starts pointing her finger at me.

'You have never met him, so you don't have the right to judge him so harshly, and so what if he is using me, maybe I want to be used' my voice is raised, and I am almost shouting.

'You sound like a slag'

I can't believe she has just called me that, how dare she. She must see the shock on my face.

'Well stop acting like one then' Jude shakes her head at me again like, I am a disobedient child.

'I am sorry Ella but you're too blind to see it because you are so wrapped up in him. The man picks you up and drops you whenever it suits him, he doesn't give a shit about you or how you feel'

By now I am crying, and Jude doesn't seem to give a shit.

'Like I said you don't even know him' I say defending Tylor again.

'No, but I sure as hell know you, and I don't like what I see anymore'

Me and Jude have argued in the past like all friends do, but she has never been so harsh with me.

I am trying not to cry but it isn't helping me at all as the tears stream down my face.

'Look at me, we have known each other most of our lives. I cannot believe you would choose a man you hardly know over our friendship'

I am not choosing between her and Tylor.

'If you have him here, then don't expect me to be here to pick up the pieces' Jude starts to put her handbag on her shoulder.

Well she is the last person I will go to now, if Tylor ever does hurt me. Why is she being so horrible?

'Ella, I mean it, if you have him here, we are done for good' she says coldly.

'Why are you doing this?' my words struggle to leave my mouth, I am an emotional wreck and can't get my head around all this.

'To protect you' Jude starts to walk towards the door.

'And if I find out he has been here, I swear to God I will knock some sense into you, myself' she closes the door behind her leaving me in a mess at the kitchen table.

How can someone be so cruel; telling her friend that she basically has no choice but to choose between their long-term friendship and a man. Who does that?

I am so hurt that Jude could be so cold and nasty.

She hasn't even met Tylor and I am sure she would like him if she even gave him half a chance, but that's not going to happen any time soon and I know it.

We are more than just long-term friends too.

Jude is like a Sister to me and the only person I had ever referred to as being part of my family.

After I finally stop crying and had a well needed smoke to calm down I try to think of the situation rationally. I have known Jude for the best part of twenty years. I have only really known Tylor for a matter of months before we lost touch. Jude has always been part of my life.

So, the choice is simple. I need to cut all ties from Tylor even if it is the last thing I want to do.

I know Jude well enough to know how stubborn she is, and it is clear she won't let this one go, without a fight.

I cannot risk losing my family when I know what she is saying is probably right.

What me and Tylor had, feels a lot more to me than it probably does to him anyway, so, I am bound to get hurt in the end. Better to be hurt again now than a few months down the line when I let myself miss him even more.

But how the fuck do I tell Tylor I can't see him?

I can't do this and feel sick at the thought of even talking to him now and I can't stand Jude at all, at the minute; but her warning is clear in my mind.

I know that if I don't stop all this now, then I will lose so much more than I think I will ever be able to comprehend.

Tylor has rung me a few times now and I need to just bite the bullet and get this over and done with, but I have no idea what I am meant to say.

I really need to ring him back so without thinking I dial his number.

'Hello this is Tylor, leave your name and number and I will get back to you as soon as I can'

Great, his phone is off!

Maybe I should leave him a message but instead I hang up, hoping he will ring me back as soon as he sees my missed call. An hour later and still no response, I feel like I am going crazy.

A walk is what I need but looking out of the window I can see the weather is about to change at any minute.

Not that I care about a bit of rain. If anything, I find it therapeutic in some ways; the amount of times I have been bitched at for not wearing a hood or owning an umbrella is crazy, and yes, I might get a bit of a cold because of it, but in that moment when the rain is pouring onto my face, I couldn't care less.

I hate this, I hate feeling like this, all I want to do is see Tylor and wrap my arms, oh, and not to mention my legs around him but I can't even speak to the man.

I hate the fact that my so-called best friend has made me feel like this.

How the hell does any of this, affect her?

I am guessing she is worried that I may move back to Belfast, but Tylor or not, that is still an open debate for me, after all my Mum lives over there, or has Jude forgotten about that.

Jude hasn't been herself since I returned, she is very snappy lately and I am starting to think she may be pregnant again, but I daren't say anything while she is in the mood she's in lately, and that's another thing; the Jude I remember would never had told me to choose between her and someone else.

There must be more to this than she is making out, to have her so worked up, and I need to find out what before I can even talk to Tylor, never mind see him again.

I head to Jude's hoping she went straight home after seeing me and if she isn't at home then I guess I will just wait, I have nothing better to do now.

The rain has just started again, and I am grateful of the sharp, chilly water as it beats of my face, though I will look like I am part of the eighties rock band 'Kiss' with my mascara running down my cheeks.

Looks like Jude is in, well at least Dan is anyway because their car is on the drive way.

I don't even want to knock on her door if I am being totally honest, but I know I haven't got a choice.

I don't want to do any of the things that today has given me so far, and I really wish I was still tucked up in my bed, obliviously content and asleep.

My cold hand stings as it collides with the wooden front door, knocking it three times.

Jude answers the door.

'Take it you spoke to him' she says all frosty.

'I have tried but he hasn't answered'

'Well you best come in' she says, I am sure she grins as I walk past her, into the living room.

'I have rung him a few times, but it just keeps ringing out' I explain.

'Well then text him, if he is ignoring you, which to me that's what it sounds like, then text him, harder to ignore words, in front of your face'

Jude has a point, but I don't think Tylor is ignoring me, although he could have easily gone in a mood with me because I didn't answer his call.

I start writing a text and try and explain that meeting up wasn't a clever idea.

Jude starts to tell me what I should put and like a puppet on a string I write what she is saying, then I stopped and looked at her when she mentioned it was best to cut all ties and let him get on with his life. I know that is the whole point of the ultimatum, and I know that if I have any sense, I would be telling my friend to mind her own business, but I feel weak and I don't want to argue. Jude is probably right, I might get hurt, but I am in my late twenties and surely old enough to decide who I can and can't see.

Even though I feel like this, I don't say a word, I just return my eyes to the screen and continue to type her words.

I am crying my heart out here, tears splashing onto my phone making it hard to type.

'You are doing the right thing, and you will find someone who won't play games with you'

I just look up at Jude and shake my head, she continues 'Ella, look at me please'

I wipe under my eyes with my fingers before looking up at Jude. For the first time since I came back, I see that look in her eyes, not sympathy as such; more emphatic, her big brown eyes looking straight into mine.

'I love you and I won't stand and watch you be hurt by this playboy'

Tylor isn't a playboy. Yes, he has had his fair share of the ladies and with his looks and charisma no one could blame him. I want to defend him, but I don't. I couldn't talk even if I tried.

‘Ready to send it? and no kisses at the end’ Jude lingers on the word no.

I just nod and push the send button.

Jude and I sit in silence for a few seconds until she moves to the sofa where I am sat and wraps her arms around me. My head finds its resting place on her shoulder as my body shakes and I sob uncontrollably, her arms squeezing me a little tighter.

‘Fuck me Ella, he must have been good in bed for you to be so worked up’

I can’t help but let out a small giggle, I try to hold it in, but it escapes my lips. That has stopped me crying at least but it sends my mind back to the last time Tylor and I were alone together, and how this man made me feel when we were connected.

Oh, Jude if you only knew the half of it I think to myself.

‘You will get over him Ella, and anyway you only knew him, for a few weeks’

I notice she is using past tense already and the man hasn’t even replied yet.

I take a deep breath and slid my bum to the back of Jude’s sofa.

‘I deserve a cup of tea’ I say, my voice is still a little shaky.

It was ten minutes later when my phone rings, it’s Tylor.

I go to pick my phone up from the table when Jude snapped at me.

‘Don’t answer it’

‘I have to’ I explained.

‘No, just wait’ she says.

Now I am confused, she wants me to end things with him over the phone, then told me to text him instead and now I am not allowed to answer his call.

'I am sure he will ring you back, let's just enjoy our tea'

I listen to her knowing that our friendship is still as thin as a tightrope. Sure, enough another ten-minutes past and he rang my phone again, this time my phone is in my hand, so Jude doesn't have the chance to try and change my mind.

Tylor is trying to reason with me, and I am coming up with any excuse. This is breaking my heart, but I am very aware of Jude's glare on me the whole time I am talking. In the end, I explain to Tylor that my family, and by that, I mean Jude and Dan don't approve of our friendship and that I need to take other people's feelings into consideration and not just my own.

Tylor bellowed down the phone to me.

'So, you are that childish, that you take everyone else's feeling into consideration but not mine and especially not your own?!'

He is completely right but I explain that if he leaves me hurt again, I need to depend on these other people, and without them I am lost. He doesn't seem to get it, and maybe Tylor has a lot of friends and doesn't see why I need Jude so much. This just adds to the list of things, that I know absolutely nothing about. Tylor was so reserved in Belfast that he never spoke about himself, so I know very little in all honesty.

I only know he has a good friend called Jonathan; because he has been at his house, on a few occasions when he's phoned me. How would he feel if John, told him he had to choose between us both? I know his friends would come before any woman and I want to say this to him, but I don't. Instead I listen to him tell me, how I need to grow a back bone and stop listening to other people.

Jude is glaring at me, she clearly thinks I am melting again. I tell Tylor that I am sorry, but that this, is all for the best.

'There is no getting through to you is there?' he sounds infuriated and I can't blame him.

I feel the tears in my eyes again and I need to get off the call before I start bawling down the phone at him.

I hope he knows I don't want to do this.

'Tylor, I am sorry, but I think we should just go our separate ways'

'Do you though, or just everyone else?' his voice is low, and I can tell I have hurt him.

'Goodbye Elouise' he says before hanging up the phone.

Now I am fucking angry and to me Jude is looking very smug stood by the fire place with her arms crossed.

I am stood here, trying my hardest not to fall in a heap on the floor and sob my fucking heart out, while she looks like she has just won an award or something.

I get a few messages one after another and I know straight away that they are off Tylor and I can tell by reading them that he is more pissed off with me than hurt and I can't blame him, he is literally on the motorway heading towards Manchester and I have just told him not to come. I would be raging too.

'Are you happy now?!' I snipe at Jude.

'No, Ella. Do you think I like seeing my best friend like this?'

I'm not actually sure anymore, Jude goes on about how I have changed but I think she needs to look in the mirror.

I walk out the room and inform her that I am using her toilet and then going home. I don't want to be anywhere near her. I have never in my life, ever thought about hitting anyone really, but all I can picture is me and her pulling chunks out of each other. This scares me a little, because I have never lost my cool and I especially don't want to lose my shit with her. I seriously need to calm the fuck down.

'Be my guest, you know where it is'

I cannot even look at her.

I am sat on the toilet, but I didn't need a pee, I just needed to get out of that room for a second, so I can at least send Tylor a message and try and explain how sorry I am. The poor man is on the motorway heading towards my house and I have told him to turn around. My hurt is starting to be replaced with guilt.

'Shit!' I accidentally say out loud.

My phone is downstairs on the unit where I was stood, I will message Tylor when I get home and hopefully by then he has calmed down a little and I can talk to him properly without Jude standing over my shoulder.

I don't want to see him, I just don't want him to completely hate me.

I can't see him, even if I wanted to, because I know Jude will never back down.

I get back down the stairs I can see Jude with my phone in her hand.

'You won't hear from him again and I have removed all traces of him from your phone' she says passing it to me.

'How dare you go through my phone' I snap.

She really is crossing the line now, I would never pick up anybody's phone and go through it.

I should have kept the password on my phone but took it off the other day when I was taking photographs. Regretting it now.

'Don't worry I didn't spend too much time looking through your photo's, I just deleted messages and calls' I look at my call log and there is no trace of him. I can feel my eyes start to well up again, so I grab my coat off the sofa.

'I cannot believe you' shaking my head at her.

'Ella, you will thank me one day'

I'm not sure I ever will but I am sick of arguing with her, I just want to go home and get back in my bed and maybe wake up next week.

'I blocked him on Facebook for you' she shouts as I open the front door.

'Goodbye Jude' my voice is subdued.

CHAPTER SEVENTEEN…

My friendship with Jude was never the same after that day. I, myself have become more secretive with my so called best friend of late, and I think Jude has noticed.

She very rarely rings me, or visits and I think ultimately the day she took control of my life was the day when she lost all control over me. I am okay though and to be honest not seeing Jude has made me go out more and socialize.

I still feel lonely and still as unsure as ever about what I should be doing with my boring and mundane life.

I was talking to my Mum on the phone last night and she misses me terribly and has asked me to at least go back to visit her. I don't know if I am ready to go back just yet.

I am only just starting to get over things and to return to the place where I met Tylor now, possibly could be the worst thing I can do.

It has been over six months since I have spoken to him.

I did unblock him on Facebook, but that was as far as I got, and I am not going to try and message him, or friend him any time soon. Too much time has passed, and I am sure he has moved on with his life, not giving me a thought in the world. I do check his newsfeed from time to time, and I am not at all surprised, to see he hasn't really been posting anything recently. Tylor wasn't really one for posting things about his life online, not like most people nowadays. He always had a secretive, mysterious edge to his character, it was one of the first things I think I had admired about him.

It is Jude's birthday this weekend and Dan has messaged me asking if I would join them. I have agreed but I am not in the mood at all.

Jude and I are talking but I find it hard to see her as my best friend nowadays, and every time we see each other it seems to be the same conversation.

On the few occasions, I have been with Dan and Jude I seen the pattern emerging again. Jude would start going on again, about how I should go out on some dates and have some fun. After the last time I tried that, does she really think it is a wise conversation. I think she must forget how much she hurt me, making me choose between herself and Tylor. I won't ever let myself be put in that situation again. Jude is the last person I want this talk with and I have told her straight.

I snapped at Jude a few weeks back and told her that she needs to stop trying to mother me and let me get on with my life. So, when she kept going on about me going out more often I made a comment about how, it was all well and good her saying that, but the last person I showed any interest to, she shut them out and made me choose between them both. I cannot forgive her, and I do know deep down that my friend did it out of love for me, but it still doesn't change the fact that my best friend controlled my life in such a cruel way. She seen how much she had broken me and couldn't care less; just as long as I didn't talk to Tylor and she was getting her own way, Jude seems to only think of herself nowadays and it is a shame, because she never used to be so cold hearted.

Maybe I am more annoyed with myself for being so foolish. Annoyed that I listened to Jude instead of following my own heart or thinking with my own head. Who's to say that me and Tylor would still be talking now anyway. Most of all, my relationship with Jude is already in ruin, it has been over six months and I am still angry with her. I have a feeling I always will be.

It is Wednesday morning and after talking with Dan, Jude starts to message me and as usual she is messaging to ask if I am taking a man with me this Saturday. I decide it was probably easier to invite someone, than to explain why I am not in the mood to take a date, let alone, even go out and Dan has offered to help me find someone.

It is Saturday and Jude asks if I will get ready at hers, like the good old days. We used to spend hours getting ready, makeup everywhere, five different dresses lay out on the bed and music blasting. It was fun. Half the time we were well on our way to getting drunk long before we were ready, but it was what we used to do. So, when Jude invites me over, I agree.

I have invited David to join us this evening, he is one of Dan's friends from work, and I already know him a little. Dan has told me a few times that his mate fancied the pants off me. What a way to make a woman feel good about herself, but I am not attracted to David really, he is a little slimy in the way he speaks, and his flirting seems creepier, rather than sexy. I do have Jude off my case for now and a man falling at my feet. I should be happy, and I know I should be, but I can just see tonight going horribly wrong, somehow.

As the evening progresses, my doubts are washed away in a sea of vodka and red bull. The drinks are free flowing, and I start to appreciate the male company for a change, as I haven't spoken properly to a man in almost half a year.

David places his hand on my leg and I don't stop him.

Is it really that bad that I am now finding him a little more attractive? By the end of the night I have let him kiss me and now I have just drunkenly agreed to meet up with him in a few days.

David seems like a gentleman and has made sure the taxi drops me off at my house before heading home himself. He wasn't pushy, so I let him kiss me in the taxi. His lips meet mine and I realize how much I have missed this interaction. I say my goodbyes and make my way to my front door, turning to wave as the taxi drives off.

CHAPTER EIGHTEEN...

It has been a good few months since me and David have started dating and at first it was fun, and a well needed distraction from Tylor but now he is starting to irritate me all the time. I never get five minutes to myself lately because he always seems to be with me. Granted most of the time he is asleep as he works nights, but even when he isn't asleep he may as well be. David acts like my home is his, which would be fine had we have been together for ages, but it has been twenty weeks, and he expects me to wait on him hand and foot just because I am not working at the minute.

He has even manipulated me into quitting smoking, and I know that it sounds like a good thing, but it just makes me more agitated and makes the simplest of tasks seem like a mountain to climb. I have tried to talk with him, but I get dismissed like my word doesn't count for shit, and the more I try to reason with him the worse I am left feeling.

I am worried all this negativity is going to make me depressed. It doesn't help that Jude and I had a big falling out last week either, and it was over something so stupid as well.

I am starting to feel really fed up and I know only too well that when I start to feel like this, something needs to change. Problem is I want everything to change.

I am in a loveless relationship and let's not get started on my sex life which is quite frankly pointless.

Is it bad that I look forward to the nights David goes to work, because I know I can at least play with myself?

That is the highlight of my sex life now; me and a piece of plastic and I honestly can't remember the last time David even touched me.

Apparently' he loves getting his cock sucked and knows I will do it whenever he asks, but to him, licking a woman is nasty. Well that is unless he is completely wasted, then apparently, it becomes bearable.

What a way to make a woman feel good about herself.

Even the night's I have managed to talk him into it, it is almost pointless. The poor man has no idea how to lick a woman and I cannot explain how frustrating it is to be turned on but to be with someone who just can't satisfy your needs, I am starting to dislike sex and surly that isn't normal.

My boyfriend is at work while I am at home watching a bit of pornography. David by the way hasn't wanted sex in over three weeks now, because he says he is stressed out with work. Whereas myself on the other hand; when I am stressed I want to be fucked hard, but he doesn't seem to get that and says that it makes me sound dirty.

Is it bad that I am fantasising about the women on the porn channel? I try and envision that they are here in this room with me. I would never be with a woman, but I do find the subtle moans in the background heightens my own pleasure. The thought of them both licking me out with as much vigor and passion as they are showing each other has my insides clenching around my fingers, I can feel the pressure build up from my groin.

My thoughts as usual swim back to Tylor.

Now that was someone who knew how to please me, and he seemed to understand not just my body but all my sexual desires, even some that I had thought I'd hidden, so well in the past. I think that Tylor knew more about me in that sense than I even understood myself, he made me want to test my own boundaries and experience new things.

I tingle all over and I need to release so bad. I am close as my legs start to shake uncontrollably so, I let them rest out flat on the sofa. With my heartrate as erratic as my breathing I can feel myself get slightly lightheaded, but I carry on with as much determination. My body raises. Fuck! I cannot take it anymore, I feel like I am about to pass out or something. Frustratingly I stop touching myself and find that I am struggling to catch my breath.

Trust me when I say that it seems even more frustrating lately, as every time I am about to climax my stupid body gives up and goes limp.

It is just past one in the morning and I need to go to bed. I plan to be up in five hours for David's return; to make his coffee and his breakfast. The arrogant prick has told me that 'it is a good way for me to show him, that I am grateful towards him for working all night long'.

Unfortunately, I was stupid enough to agree to all this at the start of our relationship and I feel obligated to continue doing so. This is yet another thing I am resenting about him lately. I set my alarm for ten past six.

I am woken by noise downstairs, so I reach beside me and look at my phone 'Shit!' it is almost seven and my stupid alarm didn't go off.

I panic and jumped out of bed pulling on my nightgown and throwing on my slippers. I quickly make my way down the stairs.

I can hear David is in the kitchen. My heart starts to race as I walk into the room behind him and instinctively I start to apologize for not already being awake, and I explain that my alarm didn't go off. David makes a comment about how he will make his own breakfast after working a twelve-hour shift, then throws in a dig about how I do fuck all around the house.

He has a cheek, the man sits on his lazy arse at work all night and never lifts a finger at home because he is a worker, and as much as he tries to say it in a nice tone I can tell it is completely forced and with intention.

He takes his coffee and toast and walks into the living room leaving me to make my own drink.

I fucking hate walking on eggshells but that is how I am feeling, and David being so cold with me makes me want to cry. I am a thirty-year-old woman, and about to cry because I have been told off, what the fuck is wrong with me lately. My period is due next week, so I put my over sensitivity down to that. Once I have finished making my coffee I walk into the living room, place my drink on the coffee table and sit down quietly.

I start to roll him a cigarette like I have done every morning since we first met.

'You should have one' he says as I pass him the cigarette and a lighter.

'No, I'm fine, you know I don't smoke anymore'.

'Go on, you look like you could do with it' he says trying to convince me that it is allowed but I just ignore him as it is obvious he is in one of his shitty moods yet again this morning.

'Did you sleep well?' he then asks me in a more sarcastic tone, than usual.

'Yes, thanks' I reply just as sarcastically as I am asked.

'No need to get arsey with me' he snaps.

Cheeky bastard says I am being arsey, he needs to take a good look at himself. I get up and walk towards the curtains, so that I can open the window, the smell of smoke lingers, and now I am not allowed to smoke myself, I notice it a hell of a lot more.

'Who was here last night' David asks.

I turn and look back at him confused and annoyed, why would he even ask such stupid questions, I make my back to the sofa.

'What do you mean by that?' I know what he is trying to say, it is obvious by his tone of voice.

'You know what I mean' he snaps.

'Clearly I don't!'

'If no one was here, why was the tv paused on fucking porn, and why is your toy left out on the sofa, if you are going to cheat while I am at work, at least clean up after yourself' he bellows.

I am more embarrassed than annoyed, ashamed that he has caught me being a dirty bitch, but to accuse me of doing it with someone else is far too much, for me to ignore.

'How fucking dare, you!' I shout. I have never wanted to hit a man but with him towering over me I just want to smack him in the face.

'I wouldn't ever cheat on anyone, never have, and I never fucking will, If I wanted to fuck someone else David, I would fuck you off first' I can feel the anger building up inside me and all I want right now, is a cigarette.

'I would be single before I ever let another man even look at me, let anyone touch me. Get it!' I snap and pick up the tobacco.

'You don't smoke' David reminds me.

'I fucking, do now, and for your information dickhead!' My voice is still raised.

'I fuck myself every night David while you are busy at work. I watch dirty bitches on the tv and fuck myself because guess what mate! you clearly don't do it for me'

David grabs the tobacco out of my hand.

'I don't believe you' he says.

'Don't believe what, don't believe that I fuck my own little pussy better than you do'

I am about to lose my temper but can't help but smile at him. David hasn't seen me this outraged before and I can see he is shocked by that stupid look on his face.

Who the fuck does he think he is to come into my house and accuse me of cheating on him.

'Stop talking with that filthy mouth!' he shouts and then sits back down forcefully almost knocking the ash tray all over the sofa.

'I will talk the way I want to' I say all matter of a fact.

'It's that book you are reading causing this' he says, 'Since you have started reading those fucking books you have been different with me'

Maybe he is right.

I started reading again a few months ago, and as far as I was concerned David didn't even notice what I was doing as he is always far too busy playing his computer all the time, but I had given him a hint into the nature of the stories were like, a few weeks back.

He had booked a few days off work as he had holiday he needed to use up but instead of doing something with his time, David just wanted to catch up on his gaming. So, I would sit with my book in my hand. We could go hours on end without talking to one another. Then one evening out of nowhere I placed my raunchy novel beside me and started to undress in front of him. David however made it clear that he was too interested in killing zombies than entertaining his so-called girlfriend. He made me feel like shit and told me I was making a complete fool out of myself. I spent the next hour in the bath and made my way straight to bed without talking to him again that evening. When I woke at seven the next morning David was as usual, still downstairs playing his stupid game.

I made us both a coffee and when I was asked about how I acted out of character the night before I just apologised and explained that the book I was reading is slightly erotic.

I can't disagree that since getting into my reading again it has changed the way I think, and probably the way I am towards him. I have been rethinking my whole life again.

Really getting into a book is my way of escaping this boring mundane life, and it may seem a little childish but with my sex life non-existent, reading the likes of filthy shades of kinky is my very own porn in my head. Surly I can't be judged for that? I am not happy with David and the more I think about it, the more it dawns on me that I don't think I have ever have been happy with him, or if I ever will be.

'What is with this new dirty side to you lately?' he asks.

I smile at him and explained this isn't a new side to me at all and that I regularly touch myself when I am on my own.

'Since when?' he asked me with that stupid shocked look on his face.

'Since I was about sixteen' I can tell I am smirking at him but don't try to stop myself.

The conversation is just reaffirming in my head what I already feel; David clearly doesn't know me at all and I am in an unhappy relationship. This wasn't part of my plan and I know something must change before I change any more of myself just to suit him. I would happily try and be a better person for someone I love, but I can never love David and I have been trying to fool myself for far too long as it is.

David moved out a few days after our argument.

He is upset more because as far as he is concerned our relationship was fine and, in his eyes, we were perfect together. He has told everyone that we had one disagreement and I blew up in his face and kicked him out.

He refused to leave me alone at first and was always texting me or trying to ring. He even had a bunch of roses sent to my door on Monday, but I put them straight in the bin. The bloke never got me flowers beforehand so why he thinks it will win me over now is beyond me. The last conversation we had, he told me that we had too much to throw away. I informed him that we have nothing, nothing to talk about, nothing in common and nothing to hope for. I have made it clear to him that the relationship is over. Even if he struggles to accept it I am not ever going to back down.

I have decided that my life is shit and I need to do something about it. I have a lot of people who live nearby that I talk to on Facebook. They have invited me out on a few occasions and even more so since I have split up with David. That's the problem with this estate, everyone knows everyone's business so as soon as the word was out that I was single again, all sorts of messages appeared in my messenger. I have found that I spent a lot of time in the evening talking to an old-school friend. Her name is Carrie, and we were close when I was in my teenage years.

It has been years since we have both seen each other properly, apart from the odd hello in passing.

Carrie and I are due to meet in town and she suggests we meet on Regent Street, the same street I once had my own little gift shop. That was almost two years ago now, when my dreams went up in flames quite literally. A hell of a lot has happened in my life since then.

Carrie and I are catching up and the conversation turns to the time I was living in Belfast and what on earth had made me come back to this dump we call home.

I talk about my Mum and siblings who still lives over there, and I also find myself speaking very highly about the man I met while I was living across the water.

Carrie is all ears and wants to know every detail, so I tell her how Tylor managed to break down a few boundaries I never thought anyone ever could get past.

I am blushing a little as I reminisce about the sex and how Tylor made me feel.

'And you stopped talking to him why?' Carrie asks.

'It was complicated' I go on to explain a little and mention Jude, and her part in me and Tylor going our separate ways.

'If you ask me, you let it get complicated Ella, by letting everyone else stick their noses in, you made it harder for yourself'

I agree with her one hundred percent.

I go on to explain how coldly I left things with Tylor and how even more frustrating it is nowadays, as Jude and I don't even speak and haven't done so in over six months.

'Why don't you get back in touch with this man?' she asks.

My heart sinks into my chair and I can't say I haven't thought about messaging him, but I have always talked myself back out of it.

'The way I left things, I very much doubt he will ever want to talk me again' I say disheartened.

'Only one way to find out' '

'This is very true'

It is almost a month later, before I finally find the courage to send Tylor a message on Facebook. I have decided that the worst that will happen, is that he will tell me to fuck off and I know I would be deserving of it.

I send a message anyway just asking how he is and trying to apologize for not staying in touch. The ball is in his court now and that is as much as I can do.

I don't even know if he checks his Facebook messages and I know he said he was never online, but you never know, as people change.

'Why did I let Jude delete his number' I stress to myself before putting my phone down and turning on the tv.

It is an hour later when I check my phone, but I wish I hadn't when I see I don't have a reply.

I am a little disheartened because Facebook does show that he has at least seen the message, but for all I know he has probably deleted it, without even looking at what it says.

I am heading to bed feeling shitty again and the way my stupid life seems to be going, everything is feeling pointless. I don't normally let myself feel so downhearted and I know being tired isn't helping so I place my head on the pillow and drift off to sleep.

CHAPTER NINETEEN…

I am in a low mood and it seems like everywhere I look I see loved up couples, it is Valentine's day after all but with that in mind I decide today is not a day for venturing outside or for looking on social media for that matter.

Valentine's day is depressing when you're on your own and I have started to realize that I am feeling lonely lately but not in a social sense as I had been out a lot.

I have forced myself into going out more often and making new friends as well as catching up with old ones. More so, I am realising that I miss the affection that only a man can give me. I don't mean in a sexual sense, but I can't deny that I do miss that side of a relationship too.

It has only been a few days since I sent the message to Tylor and I am feeling rather stupid for even sending it in the first place, but I have already told myself not to send another message, because he clearly isn't interested in talking to me and who could blame him.

I am sure he, himself is out wining and dining some lucky girl and is it bad that, that thought has a green mist forming at the front of my mind. I will put on the TV and escape into a chick flick for the afternoon.

My phone has been beeping but it is only David, trying to worm his way back into my life. Nothing he says or does will change the fact that I have no feelings whatsoever for him, even the bunch of roses he sent me haven't put a smile on my face. It's funny how it takes you to lose someone to realize what you have, well sorry David but it is too little, too bloody late, I am not interested in anyway.

Four days later I finally have a response from Tylor.

It is just before nine in the evening and I must say for the first time in ages I feel a little scared, mainly because I can see how foolish I was for even letting him go in the first place and I have no idea what he is doing with his life.

For all I know he could be happily settled down and my message might be the last thing he wants to receive.

It has taken him days to reply, which I am unsure if that is a good sign or not.

It has been over a year now since we last spoke, so I am a little apprehensive as I open his message.

Well he hasn't told me to fuck right off. Instead he has asked how I am and wants to know what I have been up to. We are messaging back and forth for over an hour and as much as Tylor is being polite, he has made it clear on how pissed off he was with me, but the message does say that even though he was angry for a while afterwards; he didn't feel the need to hold a grudge. I am so pleased and after messaging him tonight, I head to bed with the biggest smile on my face. I don't deserve him being so friendly with me, and I hope that one day I can make it up to him.

I tried to tell him how Jude had deleted his number, but he either didn't believe me or at least thought it was a lame excuse. I agree with him when he replied telling me that if I really wanted to stay in touch with him, that I could have. It has taken me forever to muster up the courage just to send that message but if I say that to him, he may think I am some head case, and I am starting to think that maybe I am.

I wake up to a good morning message off Tylor which I must say has had me in an amazing mood all day.

I am remembering how much I have missed his company and surprise myself when I ask him if he wants to meet up with me sometime soon.

Tylor rings me and it is so nice to hear his voice again, after all this time. He says that he agrees that we should meet up and tells me that he is looking forward to seeing me again. We arrange to leave it for a few weeks as Tylor would need to book the time off work. We agree that it is probably best if we both meet half way as we both remember what happened last time Tylor had tried to arrange to come and visit me.

'We can get a nice hotel or something' I am excited at the thought.

'Sounds perfect Ella, I honestly cannot wait' he says before we say our goodbyes.

We have been messaging every day, but I do still worry what it will be like next week when we meet up. I am glad to be seeing Carrie later today, so I can get all this nervous energy off my chest. I'm feeling more and more paranoid the closer we get and trust Tylor to book the first and second of April off work. Let's hope I am not his April fool's joke.

We have agreed to meet half way between where we both live and Tylor has just messaged me to tell me that he has booked a hotel room for us. Only now is it dawning on me that this is going to be the first time we are planning to spend the night together. When I lived in Belfast he always went home in the evenings and never once asked to stay the night. The thought of him seeing me asleep is worrying, I will more than likely be laying there with my mouth open catching flies and saliva running all down my cheeks, no thanks. That's not even the worst part of my paranoid thoughts; he is going to see me first thing in the morning. People call it beauty sleep, but I don't think anyone wakes up feeling beautiful.

I am overthinking this whole situation and I know I am, but I can't help it, this stupid brain of mine has a mind of its own at times.

I am completely nervous, and I worry this is all part of some elaborate get back at Ella plan and I know that, it is something I couldn't quite put past him.

You see Tylor would have normally held onto a grudge and I am honestly surprised that he has let this all go so easily.

I am so nervous, this past few weeks have flown by.

It has been over a year now since I have seen Tylor, and now I am on this train, travelling over two hundred miles to see him. I am starting to wonder what the hell I am doing, and what if he doesn't turn up? I try and put all these negative thoughts out of my mind, but I find myself looking out of the carriage window and smiling to myself; remembering how Carrie had made a comment earlier this morning about how I am being a little rash, but I like the fact that this man seems to bring out a more spontaneous side to me. Tylor gave me the excitement and rush I needed when we were last talking, and I am hoping I feel the same when we are in each other's company again.

My head is starting to hurt with all this over thinking but the more I try not to worry the harder it seems. I have sent Tylor a message to say that I am on my way, but he hasn't responded yet, it has been less than twenty minutes, so I tell myself not to stress.

I need some music, but now I am even more frustrated.

I was in such a rush this morning that I have forgotten to pick up my headphones 'Typical' I say out loud not meaning to.

Two more stops and then I will be there, and I'm still worried he isn't going to even be there when I arrive. Although he has messaged to say he is on his train as well. Maybe if it hadn't of been April fool's day today, then I would be a little more confident of this whole situation, but Tylor had picked this day due to work commitments and who am I to disagree with him. After the way, I treated him last time I am just grateful that we are even on talking terms let alone meeting up with him again after all this time.

Just as the train pulls into the station Tylor rings me.

He has taken a walk into town as he arrived earlier than expected and has asked if I minded meeting him at the Admiral pub.

'I will get a taxi to you'

Tylor is trying to give me directions but with the taxi rank right outside the station doors it seems silly to get lost when I can just get dropped off right outside.

I am fumbling about in my bag, and a small wave of panic engulfs me while I am looking for my purse, my hands are clammy, and I can hear the heartbeat in my head.

I think the nerves are kicking in now, but I find my purse and walk towards the parked taxi.

I arrive outside, and I pay and thank the driver.

I can feel my hand shake, and I am unsure if I have ever felt this nervous about meeting anyone before.

The pub looks old but well maintained from the front.

I open the big wooden doors and I am surprised, this place looks a hell of a lot bigger inside than I'd originally thought. I scan the room hoping to see that familiar face, but Tylor is nowhere to be seen. I retrieve my phone from my pocket and ring him.

'I'm sat at the back' he says so I hang up the phone and make my way towards the back of the establishment.

Fuck me he looks better than I remember!

I see him as soon as I turn the corner.

The Admiral has an elevated seating area and Tylor is stood at the top of the steps looking more handsome than ever. He is wearing a dark suit and his new shorter hair style really suits him.

Tylor smiles as I get closer and I can feel my cheeks burning as he leans down to kiss me on my cheek.

'Welcome Madame' he says as we both take as seat.

'Can I get you a drink?' he asks.

'Yes, please can I have...' Tylor cuts me off before I have chance to finish my sentence.

'I remember what you drink' he smiles, and I can't help but smile back at him.

My gaze is fixed on him as he makes his way towards the bar. Well no, let's be honest, my gaze is firmly fixed on his arse. That toned perky bitable rear end of his, is as enchanting as ever.

Once he returns to the table Tylor admits that it is good to see me and that part of him was worried I wouldn't turn up.

'Of course, I would have turned up' I say surprised that he seems almost as nervous as me.

'Well after last time my walls are up Ella, I would say I am sorry, but I am not'.

I can't blame him and if the shoe was on the other foot, I know fine rightly that I would be feeling the same, although I think I would have tried to hide it from him.

I like the fact that he was being honest and open with me and I am feeling guilty with the way things were left between us.

'I have a lot of making up to do, I know I do' I say, trying to defend my actions.

'No Elouise that is all in the past, I just wanted to make you aware of how I felt'.

I feel like shit now, but he soon gets me out of that mindset. We are laughing and catching up when Tylor places his fingers on my lips.

'Hush' he says before leaning in to kiss me.

I had almost started to forget how much of an amazing kisser this man is, so attentive and passionate that I can feel my body get weak in his embrace.

His hands fall on the small of my back, pulling me closer to him. His lips are warm and demanding, his tongue coaxing my mouth open. My heartbeat is flittering like a soaring butterfly. Tylor looks at me and grins.

'What?' I ask.

'Shall we take our things and drop them off at the hotel?' he asks giving me that cheeky half smile of his.

'That sounds like a plan, Batman!' Tylor looks at me and grins.

I am smiling more than is needed but I don't care.

The hotel room is very spacious, but I can't help but notice that he has booked a room with two single beds.

'There was a mistake with the booking' he must have read my mind.

'Yeah, yeah' I say smiling at this beautiful man, his piercing blue eyes, I assume, are penetrating my thoughts.

The beds are pushed together so I don't really have any reason to disbelieve him, but maybe the single beds were a little bit of a dig at me. It doesn't matter though because as soon as I place my bag down Tylor is behind me, his body close; his earthy smell mixed with notes of spearmint is lingering in my nose. I close my eyes and place my head back onto his torso. I am reminiscing about last year now, that earthy smell of his gets me straight away as I rest the back of my head against his chest. I have missed him.

Tylor starts to remove my coat; gently letting it fall to the floor, his fingertips running down my arms as he starts to gently blow, on my neck. I turn my head slightly and move my hair out of the way as he kisses my neck and then nibbles at it ever so slightly.

I see him grin as I start to moan softly, his hands make their way down my body making the hairs stand on end within his touch. Holding me by my hips he gently pulls me even closer to him and makes it completely obvious how aroused he is.

I feel my way behind myself and I start rubbing at his solidness through the tight suit trousers he is wearing. These trousers won't be on him long, I can tell you that much.

Tylor places his head back and I think he has closed his eyes as I feel him loosen his hold on me slightly. I need to kiss him, so I turn to face him and placed my free hand on his shoulder, my other hand running down the outside of his arm until they both meet on his belt, I start to undo it when Tylor looks down at me

'Do you want some help with that?' he asks.

Tylor takes his belt off and throws it onto the bed, and grabs hold of me, he kisses me passionately before picking me up and sitting me down on the bed. He then makes his way towards the window and I guess he is going to close the blinds as he wants some privacy but instead he just looks out of the window for a few moments. Tylor perches himself on a small round table which is situated in between the floor length windows. He gives me a massive smile; the type of smile that makes your eyes squint a little and your laughter lines more visible; the smile I have missed for far too long.

'Come here' he says in his soft Irish accent.

So, I make my way towards him walking slowly until I am close. I place myself in-between his legs and with our height difference I am at his eye level for a change.

'I have missed you' I whisper as he places his hands on my waist again.

'Your absence has been noticed'. He smiles again, biting on his bottom lip.

I know that for Tylor to even say that comment is a massive thing, but it doesn't stop my face from looking a little frustrated at his response.

'You should know me by now' he says, 'I don't tend to miss anything Ella' he can clearly see the disappointment in my eyes as I look away.

'Look my life is far too unsettled to ever let myself form attachments, I don't just mean with you but anyone in my life and if I don't form attachments then I can't miss anything, can I?' he tries explaining himself.

'I get what you mean, but it must be lonely sometimes?' I ask.

'Hell, yeah but I am used to it'.

Tylor pulls me closer to him again and leans in to kiss me. He runs his tongue slowly across my lower lip, enticing a small moan to escape through my breath. I am instantly fighting the urge to wrap my arms around him, pulling him even closer to me. Tylor places his hand gently in my hair, his lips push against my own, his tongue seeking entry and encouraging my lips to part and I accept him into my mouth, he is just as consuming as I remembered.

I am lost in this moment, he is captivating me, and I think he knows it. Just then the table makes a cracking sound; and before I know it, it has landed on the floor taking Tylor with it. I laugh hard, but still check to make sure he hasn't hurt himself. The roaring laughter from both of us fills the high vaulted hotel room.

Tylor is clearly fine, but my stomach hurts, I haven't laughed like this in such a long time.

I place out my hand to help him, still trying to hold my laughter inside.

'Well that killed the mood' he says getting back on his feet and dusting himself down.

'Want to go get some food? You may need the energy later when you know what I have planned for us' his voice is very domineering and I let out a small yelp as his hand collides with my bum cheek.

I do wonder what he has planned.

My mind is going crazy and I think it is noticed as Tylor winks at me and gives me that half smile that he does so well. I am hungry, but I am still nervous around Tylor and want a drink more than anything.

'What do you fancy?' I ask

'You' Tylor winks at me.

'I meant food, what do you want to eat?'

'Ella, I know what you meant but I stand by my first answer, I fancy you and would like to eat you all night long if you let me'

I can feel myself go red on the spot, but that thought does have my mind wondering just how long he could last eating me out, I know my body would never last a whole night, but I am willing to give it a go.

'Oh, Tylor, I will let you do that anytime'.

'Oh, I know you will, you don't really have a choice in the matter'.

Is that right, I think I like this 'being told' business, well I at least know my body does as I feel my insides tighten as soon as the words leave his lips. We are chatting for ages while we wait on our food, I have decided to go for a burger because I'm not feeling all that hungry now that we have sat down, though my drink seems to be going down very quickly indeed.

I tell Tylor about how I have started writing and he seems impressed. He then tells me about how his teaching job had fallen through but how it didn't stop his from doing his artwork part time. He says he had moved from Belfast for a guaranteed job and it turned out that there wasn't a job after all.

'So, what did you do?' I ask, not really knowing what to say.

'I got a normal shop job for now, but I have applied for a few places and I have interviews coming up'

'Do you ever wish you hadn't have left?'

I am surprised when he says that he doesn't regret any decision he has ever made, and that he knows he would have left eventually.

'But that's not to say I don't miss my family'

'That's understandable' I say as the waitress makes her way to the table with our food, we thank her, and Tylor asks if I want another drink.

'Yes please'

I am nibbling away at my burger, while Tylor finishes his in as little mouthfuls as possible. I am guessing he is hungry.

'You still don't eat much' he says noticing my appetite is as poor as ever.

'I do, I am just a little nervous around you still'

I can feel my face starting to go a lovely shade of red as I look back down at my food.

Tylor wraps his arm around my shoulder and pulls me in closer, so he can plant a kiss on my face. He works his way to my ear and bites down.

'Don't be nervous' he whispers before kissing the sensitive void under my lobe.

I shudder from head to toe.

Oh, good God, I want him to fuck me so badly.

I close my eyes, to take in this moment completely.

I hate how nervous I am feeling.

'You have nothing to be nervous about around me, you should know that by now'.

'It's okay for you, Mr. oh, so confident' I say smiling back at him.

I find myself just staring into his eyes for what seems like ages. He really does have the most amazingly blue eyes which seemed to be more saturated with colour when he smiles. I lean closer to kiss him properly, the fact that he smells like pulled pork doesn't bother me in the slightest. Barbeque flavoring turns my stomach at the best of times, but I just want to feel his lips against mine. Instantly I feel better, feeling him pressed against me, feeling his warmth again. I really have missed this man more than I care to let on. I let out a small noise, not a moan as such, but not too far off it as his tongue laps against my lips, teasing my mouth open again, he then stops and just giggles at me like we are two teenagers.

'We best stop with our public displays of affection otherwise Miss Roberts, I will bend you over this table right now and bury myself deep inside you'

'Well I didn't plan to get arrested on this visit, so I have to agree with you' I reply biting on my lower lip.

Although the temptation to let him fuck me here and now is now more overwhelming than ever.

'Come on, let's find that karaoke bar near the hotel'.

The walk is exactly what is needed to calm down my sexual impulses. As we arrive outside the pub, I look across the street and realize we are opposite our hotel.

'It's ideal here, with the hotel just there' I say pointing across the road.

'That is why I said about coming here, doesn't matter how drunk we get, when we only have to stagger across the road'.

Typical Tylor, everything is planned perfectly.

The bar is busy, and I am pleasantly surprised when Tylor put his name up to sing.

'I almost forgot you could sing'. I confess.

Tylor blushes for the first time this evening and it makes me feel more comfortable.

'I can't sing but I have had a drink, so I don't really care'.

Well I know that is a lie, he used to sit with my guitar and sing away when we lived in Belfast, but I just smile at him. We order our drinks and make our way to a small round table, that makes me giggle as I remind Tylor we have a broken table to contend with back at the hotel. He says he will fix it, but I don't see how he can, not unless he has packed a hammer in his bag and if that is the case, I would want to know why.

Tylor's name is called up, but he looks nervous as hell.

He needn't be worried as his confidence grows during the song as he starts to belt out the chorus of the plain white T's hit song. Most of the customers are looking over at him, and almost everyone in the bar is singing along.

My face is hurting from all the smiling, he looks like a natural on the stage and I am feeling a little proud as he makes his way back towards me and kisses me on the cheek before walking over to the bar.

'That was awesome!'

Tylor then heads to the bar to receive his free drink.

'If you want a shot, you best get up to sing' he says before necking the liquid and sucking on a slice of lime.

There is no way on this earth I am going to get up and sing.

It is almost midnight when we make our way back across the road to the hotel. Tylor said he couldn't wait to get me into the hotel room, but as soon as the elevator door closes he has me pinned up against the wall, with his hand gently around my neck. He knows I hate anything around my neck and I can tell he is just doing this to see how far he can go, I let him have his way for now, but I will remind him how much I hate it later.

'All I have thought about for days is having my wicked way with you' he whispered in between kissing my shoulder and lower neck.

The elevator door opens, and Tylor released his hold of my neck and places his hand in mine. I smile at him.

'When you get into the bedroom, I want you to strip' he says in a very assertive tone.

'I don't think so' I raise my eyebrow as I look up at him.

'I wasn't asking Ella, I was telling you' he somchow says it with a straight face. I stop a few feet from the door and he turns around to look at me.

'Are we trying to take control?' he gives me his best half smiled and winks before slapping my arse as hard as he can.

'Fuck! you are going to pay for that' I say holding onto my burning cheek. He turns me on so much.

'I think I like you being domineering. Should I call you sir?' I can't sound any more sarcastic even if I tried, but he just smiles at me.

'That's good because you don't have a choice, you have to call me sir now that you have put it in my head' he opens the door to our room.

'Now strip!' this time his voice is more demanding, he defiantly isn't asking me.

I can feel my heart thumping hard which isn't helping my irregular breathing. Tylor hasn't even touched me yet, but I can feel the sexual pleasure building up inside and my opening starts to tense as I slowly remove my dress followed by my tights.

Tylor has made his way to the arm chair, having a small giggle to himself at the now lopsided table beside him. He turns back to face me and looks intently at me stood in my black lace underwear.

'I told you to strip woman' his tone still as forceful. I roll my eyes at him.

'Did you really just roll your eyes at me?!' he snaps and raises to his feet again.

'I did' I say all matter of fact.

I know for a fact that has pissed him off a little.

My heart is almost jumping out of my chest as he makes his way towards me. He looks pissed, like not the playful oh I am in charge now, but more like I have offended him. His is in front of me, looking down at me when he pulls me towards him, by my waist. I can feel his hardened manhood pressing against my core.

'Don't ever roll your eyes at me again, not if you don't want punished for it'.

I close my eyes thinking he is leaning in to kiss me.

'Fuck!' I feel a sharp sting as he squeezes the life out of my nipple.

He smiles at me before letting go and kissing me passionately, his one hand tangles in my hair as the other pulls me in closer.

'You needed punished' he says softly before turning his back to me again and making his way back to the arm chair.

'Oh, is that the way it is tonight?' I ask, slightly shocked.

'You know you like it'.

I really cannot deny that right at this moment I feel turned on more than ever. Apart from a throbbing nipple, all I can feel, is the sexual pressure rising inside me. I feel myself getting damper by the second.

'Now strip' this time is voice seemed a little softer.

Maybe me yelling out in pain caused a little bit of guilt to form in this man's mind but somehow, I doubt it.

I am now stood naked in the middle of the room.

Tylor has told me to face the wall and makes it clear that I am not allowed to look behind me, so I do as I am told.

With my eyes fixed on a small black mark by the doorway, I can hear him behind me removing his clothes.

I am a little apprehensive as I hear him removing his belt.

I like this control, but the thought of being slapped with a belt isn't sitting well.

Would he whip me with a belt?

More importantly, would I enjoy it?

My nipple still stings a little but I daren't try and deny how much it turns me on. I want nothing more than to feel him deep inside me, but I have a feeling that isn't going to happen for a while yet.

Tylor always has a plan, and I have no idea what he has planned for us tonight in that creative mind of his.

It does worry me, but only a little.

'Do you trust me?' he asks.

His voice seems closer and as tempted as I am to look, I decide to keep facing the wall. Do I trust him? Well that's a big question isn't it, and not one I am going to answer out loud. The fact that I am naked, facing the wall I think says it all.

I almost jump out of my skin as Tylor gently runs his finger down my spine.

'Your skin is so soft' he whispered in my ear. I can feel my whole body start to tingle. I lean my head back to look at him. 'coco butter'.

Tylor raised his eyebrow as I smile at him, I know I should be facing the wall, but I need to defy him sometimes.

'Nice to know, but did I say you can look at me?'

I am feeling tortured and all I can think about is how much I want to pounce on him. I feel the pressure building up inside me, those butterflies, are now more like a swarm of fireflies, heating me up from the inside out. Tylor's fingertips traced their way around my pelvic bone. He pulls my body close, making sure I can feel his arousal pressed up against my lower back. I cannot help but moan in pleasure and tilt my head back again.

This time I am keeping my eyes closed, so Tylor can't tell me off, for looking at him.

'You can look at me you know' his tone is soft and gentle.

Well make up your mind.

I am in my very own world of Tylor, he mesmerizes me. I look straight at him, his swirly blues staring straight back at me, has me captivated in an instant. I close my eyes again and breathe in deeply; taking in his natural scent, that I cannot get enough of.

'Look at me please' he says quietly so I do what he asks.

'Do you have any idea how much you turn me on?'

I can see clearly how aroused he is, his pulsating manhood gives it away. I smile at him.

'I think I get the idea, kind of hard to miss Tylor'

I feel myself blush as I look down at this sexy beast of a man and for tonight at least, his attention is completely on me. I am turned around with my back pressed against the cold wall as Tylor starts to lower himself onto his knees, I look down at him and he gives me a cheeky smile before burying his head into my groin.

'Oh, my. Someone is very turned on' he says admiring how wet I am.

'What can I say Tylor, you have this effect on me'

Before I know it, he is lapping against my clitoris, putting just enough pressure, that I raise to my tip toes.

Tylor then places his fingers inside me.

Tylor starts to push harder with his hand while keeping his tongue circling my feminine hood. I am not sure I can take much more as he makes me cum. My moans are normally very quiet, but I can't help it, I let out a loud, stretched out moan as he removes his fingers and starts kissing my body gently. I tingle all over and my legs feel like jelly as I lower myself back onto the flats of my feet.

He then gets up and makes his way towards the armchair by the window, I follow him because he hasn't told me to stay where I am.

'Did I say you can move' he asks.

'I don't care if you did, it is my time to please you'

I am glad he doesn't argue as he lowers himself into the chair.

'And how do you plan to do that' he says with his hand firmly placed around his hardened cock.

'Might be best if I show you'

I move myself onto my knees, in between his legs.

I start by removing his hands and placing them either side, on the arms of the chair, and give him a don't move look without the need to speak any words.

Tylor nods at me so I guess he knows the score.

I then run my nose against his shaft, making my way higher as slowly as I can manage. He lets out a small moan but that isn't good enough, so I place my tongue on the end of him, licking up and down. He twitches, and I can't help but look up and smile at him.

'Oh, fuck yes' he says placing his head back and closing his eyes.

That's better. Now I am going to really make him moan I think to myself before placing my mouth around the full width of his hardness. I place myself lower, taking more and more of him with each forward motion. Tylor's legs are starting to tense up and I can feel his main vain throbbing in my mouth. I place my hand around his balls and gently caress them while my other hand is teasing myself. I know Tylor loved me touching myself before but last time I did that more for him. I feel the need to touch myself even more because with each moan that escapes his mouth, I can feel my own body responding. I feel myself tingling all over, the fireflies in my chest are causing an electrical surge to spread across my back and down my spine.

I just came a little and it makes me smile to myself.

I am soaking wet as I start to suck on him a little harder and faster.

Tylor places his hand in my hair in an attempt, I am guessing to hold my head in place, but he should remember that I refuse point blank to swallow.

I stop what I am doing and look up at him, his hand still tangled in my hair.

'I can't swallow you know that' I say reminding him.

'I know Ella, I am not ready to cum yet'

So, I carry on teasing him, my hand has moved from his balls and now squeezing the base of his shaft as I try to take more of him, but to no avail. I start to gag so gently remove is cock from my mouth and start to play with him instead. My hands are doing a very good job at mimicking my insides.

'You will make me cum, if you carry on doing that' Tylor says, his voice sounding short of breath.

'Do you want to cum?' I ask.

'Not until I have fucked you silly' Tylor pulls me up towards him and kisses me gently.

'Now get on the bed!' his demanding tone has reappeared and fuck me he sounds sexier than normal.

'Yes sir'

I do as I am told but I am soon flipped over onto all fours and he is pressing hard on my clit. His fingers enter me, and I feel myself tighten around him again. I am loving the way he treats my body, with pure lust, but with a gentle side too, even when he is being a domineering arse.

'You do not know how much I have been thinking about this' he says before kissing my back.

I then feel him line himself up with my body as he forces his self, inside me. Tylor pushes harder, causing my body to lean forwards, not expecting him to pound me so hard.

'Oh, fuck' I moan.

Tylor starts to pound even harder, his grip on my hips increasing with his speed, I am about to cum again as I feel him explode inside me. His moan is long and drawn out as I am pulled up towards his chest.

'Please don't say Oh, fuck' he whispers,

'Something about the way you say it makes me want to cum far too quickly' he explains.

'Oh fuck! I am sorry sir' I reply smiling at this beautiful man.

Tylor starts to fuck me some more, surely, he has just released and can't carry on, but that doesn't stop him and before I know it I am screaming out in pleasure as he hardens again inside me. He places his hand in my hair and gently tugs it.

'You can - pull harder - than that' I say in between being thrusted forward again.

'Fuck me Ella' he moans.

'You really are a bad girl' he says sounding surprised.

'I – am – a – good – girl' his speed increasing as I try and speak.

I feel his hand makes it way towards the front of me as he starts to tease my womanly organ, keeping to the same pace as he is fucking me. I am about to release all over him, I can feel it all building up inside me. Tylor must feel it too, as he grips my hips and pulls me in closer, our bodies crashing off each other and my body failing me as I finally let go, all over Tylor and the bed.

'Fuck me woman you are something else' he says collapsing on the bed beside me, his breathing is as heavy as my own.

I am lay on his chest while his fingers trace their way through my hair. He is the only man who has ever held me like this and I could easy fall asleep like this, but I am conscious that my head will get heavy on him. I lift my head and I am awarded with a kiss.

'Are you not comfortable?' he asks.

'I am but guessing you might not be if I fall asleep'

'That's silly, you weigh nothing, but my back is killing me' he squeezes me into his chest before releasing his warmth from me.

These mattresses are a little softer than I am used to, and Tylor was lay across the gap of the two beds. I am surprised he hasn't fallen through. That thought has me smiling to myself. Tylor gives me a light gentle kiss and we both say our goodnights, he then turns on his side and I find myself tracing my hand over his masculine back.

'That feels amazing' he says, 'I could let you do that all night'

Within ten minutes he is fast asleep, and I turn over and drift off myself, feeling very content with my naked state.

CHAPTER TWENTY…

I wake up to Tylor in the bathroom and I am guessing the flush must have woken me. I am lay here in bed just looking up at the ceiling when I hear the en-suite door open.

'Good morning beautiful'

I roll onto my side to see him better and instinctively bite on my lower lip. He is stood in the door way, completely naked and fully aroused.

Oh, I could look at this man all day long.

'Good morning' I reply as he starts to walk towards me.

I sit up and he leans down to kiss my forehead.

Tylor then holds out his hand, I place mine in his, as he throws the covers off me. I am not cold, but my body notices the change as the hairs on my arms stand on end and my nipples harden. He looks down at me with a smile. No one has ever looked at me this intently, his eyes then fix on mine.

'I have run you a bath, but I think I need to fuck you first' he grins. 'you cannot look this fucking hot and think that I won't notice'

'Why, thank you' I reply shocked at first.

He really is such a gentleman, either that or he is trying to tell me I smell.

The bubble bath aroma fills the room.

Tylor is staring straight at me.

Shit! what must I look like with yesterday's makeup on and my hair everywhere?

He said I look hot, but I am sure he has only said that to be nice. I don't have time to even sit up when I am pulled to my feet. Tylor wraps his arms around my waist and kisses me, his facial hair is rubbing against my nose as I stand on my tip toes to reach him better. I love how attentive his kisses seem, but I am sure my morning breath is delightful, whereas his breath is fresh and minty.

Although, I still kiss him back with just as much passion as he is giving me. He stops and looks directly in my eyes, I am feeling a little shy again, but Tylor just smiles at me and bites down on his lower lip.

I wish I could see through his eyes, but I am content with the sight I am seeing in front of me.

'I am sure I look a complete state' I say bowing my head and tracing his perfect chest, my hands fall on him.

I can feel his heartbeat against my hand, it is beating as fast as mine.

'Well you do look a state, but that doesn't stop me wanting to have my wicked way with you'

Cheeky sod, he is meant to say something like, don't be silly or you still look good to me. I think it is one thing I am starting to admire about him. Tylor says it how it is, no matter the mood or situation.

'Now if you don't mind I am going to slide myself deep inside you' he leans down towards me kissing that sensitive area behind my ear. I feel the hairs on the back of my neck stand on end as a small moan escapes my lips.

'Oh, I don't mind at all' I say tilting my head to the side giving him more room.

I am turned around with my shins against the base of the bed and my back pulled straight against his chest. He starts by kissing my neck again before lowering my body slowly, so my front is on the mattress. Tylor uses his knee to part my legs.

He traces his hand down my spine, and I shudder.

I can feel the head of his cock slowly tease my opening and I am already damp with the anticipation.

I feel tight as he invades me, filling up every part of my insides. I close my legs a little to make me tighten around him even more, and I can't help but smile as he lets out a big moan before saying my name and increasing his speed. My legs are moved apart again and this time I don't resist. My stomach is clenching as he pounds me harder and harder with each thrust of his hips.

'Oh, fuck I am about to cum' I say quietly.

'You woman, need to stop telling me this'

I can feel the grip on my hips tighten, my breathing getting deeper as Tylor pulls me closer to him, pushing himself inside me as deep as physically possible.

Tylor lets out a long drawn out moan before releasing his hold and tracing his fingertips over my lower back.

'Now you do need a bath' he says on a giggle.

I hear his hand connecting with my arse cheek, but it doesn't sting. I am even feeling a little disappointed that it didn't sting even just a little. I am all sweaty and that bath is so welcoming. Tylor leads me to the door.

'Your bath Madame' his voice is husky and deep, and I just smile at him as I make my way to the bathroom door. He perches himself against the door frame.

I am about to close the door on him, when I am pulled in for a kiss.

'Though you really do need to brush your teeth' he smiles.

I just shake my head at him and start to close the door over. Tylor leaves me to enjoy my bath. I know in an hour or so this will all be over, so I have a wash in record time.

I know I shouldn't be thinking like this, but I don't want today to end. It has been a long time since I have felt so good about myself and I know that it is down to him. Tylor is kind and gentle but also rough and ready, an almost perfect mix if you ask me.

'That was quick' he says surprisingly as I re-enter the room in nothing but a towel.

Tylor passes me a coffee and has rolled me a cigarette.

'Fancy putting something on, so we can go out for a smoke?' he asks.

'Sounds like a plan' I stop myself from adding the batman on the end of that sentence but smile to myself remembering the time when we first met.

It is crazy but even though we haven't seen each other in such a long time, I feel closer to him now.

Maybe that is just because we have spent our first night together.

I chuck on a pair of leggings and Tylor passes me his jumper.

'Will be warmer than that, thin thing' he says pointing to my lace top I was planning on wearing today.

'Why, thank you' I can feel my cheeks are starting to ache with all this smiling.

It is colder outside than I anticipated, and I am grateful of his warm woolen jumper.

'It's only just gone ten' I say thinking it is a lot later in the morning.

'I know, breakfast time' he replies with a massive grin on his face.

'Oh, have we worked up an appetite?' I ask.

He smiles at me, while rubbing his stomach.

'You know me, I love my food, just wish you did too' he says nudging me with his elbow.

'I love food Tylor, I am just a fussy bitch'

'Oh, I know that'

My train isn't till twenty-past one, but we need to check out at twelve. We finish our smoke and head straight to the restaurant for breakfast. Tylor orders a big fry up, while I just stick to a bacon sandwich and a pure orange juice.

'You hungry?' he asks.

I am but these nerves have creeped in again as he looks at me, I really wish I knew what went on in that beautiful mind of his. I nod but my stomach is doing summersaults again and I hope I can eat.

'What are you thinking about?' I ask trying to break the awkward silence that is creeping in.

Tylor looks in a world of his own and I cannot judge his expression.

'How I want to take you upstairs and make you not forget me in a hurry'

'Oh, I cannot see me forgetting anytime soon' I confess 'I have had an amazing time and I don't really want this day to end'

'I know what you mean' Tylor looks a little gutted himself.

'Sure, we can arrange something again soon' I say.

He smiles at me and takes hold of my hand.

'Yes. That would be nice, maybe I can come see you next time'

I agree, knowing that I won't let anyone else have a say in my life again, not after last time anyway.

I promised myself that I am the only person who will make decisions about my life, after all I am thirty years old and old enough to make my own mistakes and triumphs.

Breakfast is served, and I am enjoying my sandwich more than I expected.

'Is it nice?' Tylor asks with a mouthful of food.

I laugh and nod my head at him.

'Think I needed this' I say taking another mouthful.

'Nice to see you eat for a change'

'I'm sure'

'As much as you look sexy in my jumper, I am going need to take it home' Tylor says as we enter the elevator to head back to our room.

I smile to myself knowing that the last time we were in this lift, I was pinned to the wall. Is it bad that I want him to do it all over again? I start to remove his jumper when I hear him giggle.

'I didn't mean right now, but if you want to strip, I won't stop you'

'I am sure you won't either' I nudge him with my elbow as the elevator doors open.

'I will have you naked in a few minutes anyway' he says confidently.

'Oh, is that, right?' I ask.

My body has taken notice and I am feeling turned on again. He is welcome to do with me what he pleases, but I won't admit that to him. Tylor opens the door to our room and as soon as I enter I am pushed up against the back of the door, closing it shut. His hand find's the lining of my underwear, he traces the outline. I can feel myself start to throb and as I look down I see his own trousers are looking uncomfortably tight as well.

'I really don't like leggings' he whispers

'Then we best take them off' I bit my bottom lip knowing that the inevitable is about to happen.

The good thing about leggings; is how stretchy they are, and Tylor is soon pulling my waist band from my body and using his fingers to move my knickers out of the way.

'I think you are right' he says giving in and standing back a few steps.

Tylor is stood with his legs parted slightly and his arms folded across his chest.

'I am waiting' he says impatiently.

I remove my leggings, but I keep my underwear on, if he wants them off he can do it himself.

'And the rest' he says now seeming more impatient.

'That's your job' I say firmly.

'If that's the case, get here' oh, his tone is demanding again and as much as I don't want to piss him off, I need to stand my ground a little.

'You come here' I smile at him as he makes his way towards me.

'If you don't want them ripped off I suggest you do as you are told'

'As I am told?' I say questioning him.

'I know you secretly like it' Tylor starts kissing the nape of my neck.

I really do like this assertive side to him, but at the same time I am unsure how far this will go, so I just grab hold of his hand and place it on the lining of my knickers.

'You want me to rip them off' he asks sounding slightly shocked.

'Yes, but are you going to replace them?' I ask.

'No, if I rip them, then it is your own fault, don't say I didn't warn you'

Tylor really is something else. I don't know what is wrong with me. Any other man who would dare to tell me what to do, would get a swift kick in the bollocks, but not him. For some strange reason, this controlling side to him has my mind swimming as much as my body.

I decide to remove my underwear myself but while I am bent down I make sure my face is level with his groin. I am teasing his erection through his trousers with my lips pushing rather firmly against the fabric.

Tylor gently pulls me up level to him and lifts me, so that my legs are around his waist and my arms draped over his shoulders.

'I had forgotten how little you weigh' he says as he walks us both over towards the two single beds.

'Now I am going to taste you' he says before lowering me onto my back.

I am lay with my knees up and legs open as he starts to lift my top.

'I want to keep this on' I explain.

'I will let you have your own way for now' he replies.

Tylor kisses my stomach and I am pleased when he doesn't try to lift my top higher. He knows how insecure I am about my body and I am glad when he doesn't push the matter. His lips feel soft against my skin and I find myself holding onto his shoulders wanting him to lower himself.

I am rewarded with that half smile only he can do, then I feel his finger slide inside me. I can't talk, all words have left my mind, so I just smile back at him.

'I do like this effect I have on your body' he sounds very self-assured.

I also like the effect he has on me and slightly annoyed that my body reacts so well to his touch. The last thing I want is to be so wet, that I loosen up. His lips start to etch lower until he finds my clitoral hood, he is licking me gently while his fingers are deep inside me. I moan out in pleasure which has him adding a little more pressure.

Oh fuck! I can feel my legs starting to tighten and spasm as he runs his tongue down lower until he reaches my opening. He removes his fingers and replaces them with his tongue, lapping up my juices. His fingers invade me again, he pounds me harder and faster.

'Cum for me Ella' I hear him say before I let out a big deep breath.

My legs shake uncontrollably, and I am feeling a little embarrassed at the mess he has helped me make.

Now it is my turn. I grab Tylor by the waist and pull him into me to kiss him. I can taste myself off his beard but that doesn't stop me, if anything it just added to this all-consuming lust I am feeling for him.

'My turn' I say slightly panting.

'Be my guest' Tylor takes his trousers and boxers off and lays on the bed, sorting out all the pillows behind his head.

Once I see he is comfortable I get on all fours and slowly make my way up the bed. Tylor's eyes are closed as I run my fingertips up the inside of his legs. I see his shaft twitch as I trace my fingers around his groin. My mouth starts to water as my face gets closer to him. I use the tip of my tongue to tease the full length of him. I look up and Tylor is watching me, so, I place my mouth around him, his head flies back again. He lets out a small and I can feel him pulsate as I force myself lower onto him. I have never been able to go deep and never really tried but I am finding myself almost forcing myself as lower as I can without of course gagging on him. I only have a small mouth, so I am struggling to get more than just his tip inside my mouth comfortably, but I keep trying to lower myself even more.

Tylor is moaning in pleasure as I gain pressure and suck on him harder. My tongue is lapping against his head and it just makes me want to give his manhood as much attention as I can. I place my hand firmly around the base of his shaft when he warns me that I am about to make him release. I am so tempted to keep my mouth where it is, but I know just the smell of his juices will turn my stomach, so I move onto my knees and continue to play with him until his creamy mess covers his stomach.

I smile to myself loving the fact that I have just made him make a mess over himself. Tylor reaches for the towel of the floor beside us.

'I should make you lick it up' he jokes.

'Never' I scrunch my nose up in disgust and Tylor shakes his head and smiles at me.

'Never is a long time, I am sure I will trick you one day'

He has got another thing coming if he believes I will ever swallow, it is possibly the only rule I have given myself.

I just know that even the thought of it; has my stomach turning and my instincts are to hug the toilet seat.

We are lay in each other's arms for what feels like ages, when Tylor looks down at his watch and sighs.

'We best think about getting ready' he says, 'We need to check out in half an hour'

Just a few more minutes. I am totally relaxed and feeling sleepy after that orgasm, but I know he is right. My clothes are scattered all over the room.

'What time is your train' he asks.

'Just after one'

'Mine is just before two so I will stay at the platform with you till your train arrives'

'Thank you' I say as he cuddles me.

'Do you fancy a coffee or pint before we head to the station?' I ask.

'Yeah, why not'

Tylor gets up and starts getting dressed, I want to just lay here and watch him, but I know I should get up and get ready myself, I am pulling the best sulky face I can to show how disgruntled I am, but Tylor just laughs at me and tells me to stop being a dick. Well it was worth a try.

Were at the train station and with over half an hour still to wait. So, decide to head to the café on the other platform. Tylor orders our drinks while I grab us a table. The coffee isn't all that and nowhere near as nice as I had hoped but I drink it anyway.

We have arranged to try and meet up again soon I am a little gutted that I am having to head home, but it was lovely while it lasted, and I am grateful of the time we have spent together. I can tell I am over thinking again and I give myself a mental telling off.

'You okay' Tylor asks clearly noticing I am miles away.

'I am fine, I have just been thinking about how glad I am we met up'

'I know what you mean' he says placing his hand on top of mine.

'Next time let's not leave it as long' I can feel my hands start to clam up.

You would think the nerves would have subsided by now, but clearly not. I hate saying goodbyes and I am kind of wishing my train to hurry up; it's cold today and I have noticed Tylor keeps looking at his watch, so I have a feeling he is thinking the same as me.

'Will you ring me when your home?' he asks breaking the silence.

'Of course, I will, it's only a two-hour journey'

I don't know why I said that, he knows how long the train takes because he made a comment yesterday that we really did choose a midway point to meet up because his train takes the same amount of time.

'I know it is' he says with that big grin of his 'it really has been good to see you Ella' he says kissing me on the top of my head and pulling me in close to him.

'And you, I kind of don't want to leave' I confess.

'Oh, please do, I need to catch my own train home' he says jokingly.

'As much as I have enjoyed this weekend, I have a life to get back to and so do you' he reminds me.

CHAPTER TWENTY ONE…

I message Tylor just as my train gets into Piccadilly station just to tell him that I am home safe, and he replies telling me that he has just got off the train himself. We text back and forth a few times and I can't help but have a big smile on my face and I am sure half the passengers have noticed too. A few people have smiled back at me as I exit the train and I feel amazing.

My good mood hasn't gone unnoticed when I bump into Jude as I make my way through town. We haven't seen each other in months so no doubt this is going to be awkward. Out of everyone I could have bumped into. It is her. Just my luck I mutter to myself.

'What has you beaming so much?' her voice is high pitched and full of excitement.

'Nothing' I say not really wanting this conversation.

'Where are you going?' she looks down at my case.

I want to tell her all about Tylor but at the same time I know how judgmental she has been, so I lie straight to her face. Normally I would feel bad lying to anyone, but she seems to forget that we aren't as close nowadays and she really has no right to have an opinion in my life.

'I have been visiting friends, a much-needed break'

'Who?' she asks, 'I want to hear all about it but first we need coffee' she says pointing to Starbucks.

I agree but, in all honesty, I just want to go home.

Meeting up with Tylor and talking about my passions has made me keen to start thinking of myself and there is something about spending time with Tylor has made me want to attempt to be creative.

'So, who is he?' Jude asks with her mouth full of chocolate éclair.

'Who said it was a he, I went to see' I am sounding more defensive than I had hoped.

'Your face gives it away'

I really can't be doing with her damping my mood, but I am hoping yesterday's trip happens again, so I decide to bite the bullet and just confess all to her.

'Oh, if you must know I met up with Tylor'

'You did what?!' she snaps.

'I met up with Tylor and I am sorry Jude, but it has nothing to do with you'

I can see the vain on the side of her head appear, this is the indication that she is pissed with me, but I made the mistake last time of listening to her opinion and I refuse to let her manipulate me again.

'None of my business, are you for real?'

She off again and I am half shutting off to her ranting. Didn't take long, we lasted a whole five minutes before she is playing mother goose to me again. This is why; we fell out in the first place.

'Are you even listening to me. Ella, you are crazy if you start seeing him again and I told you last time I won't stand around and watch you get hurt'

'Then feel free to leave' I snap.

Fuck, did I just say that to her, wow I am growing some balls. Jude doesn't move, instead she piles more cake into her fat face. I did wonder if she had gained a few pounds and now I know it is highly likely.

I get up from my seat and grab my case.

'I just wish you would be happy for me' clearly, she isn't.

I can hear her muttering as I walk away but I refuse to look back. I am livid, a complete contrast to how I was feeling less than an hour ago, but I am glad I stood up for myself, finally.

My place is trashed, and I had forgotten I had left it in such a state, but the housework can wait for now because all I want to do now is put on my night clothes and fall into a heap on my bed. I am not tired but can feel myself slowly starting to drift off. I know it's early still, I am lucky if it is even seven in the evening, but I don't care.

Jude has really dampened my mood and I am really wishing I hadn't bumped into her.

I wake to the sound of my phone beeping. It is pitch black outside, so I have slept for a few hours at least. With one eye, open and the other firmly shut I can see that I have two messages, so I open the folder.

Its Tylor, he has sent a message to say that he was planning on getting an early night and that he hasn't stopped smiling since he got back.

I look at the time and see it is almost one in the morning, my body automatically yawns, and my eyes fill with water. That hurt my mouth.

Do you ever yawn so hard that it hurts your face?

I seem to keep doing it today, maybe having Tylor's cock so deep down my throat has cause this, and I smile, it's a dirty smile but I like it.

The second message is off Tylor as well wishing me a goodnight. I type a reply telling him that I have been smiling myself all day and that he must of warn me out because I had fallen asleep as soon as I got home.

Lazy shit he replies, I hope I haven't woke him.

I wish him a goodnight and once he has replied I place my phone on charge and roll over to get comfortable and did I mention this isn't the most comfortable bed in the world, but I am too sleepy to even care and drift off to sleep with a smile still on my face.

CHAPTER TWENTY TWO…

I am doing my much-needed housework when my friend Carrie rings me. I only spoke to her a few hours ago so wondering what she must have forgotten to tell me earlier.

'Have you seen what that woman has put on your Facebook?' she asks.

'No who do you mean?' I haven't looked on Facebook in a few days now, so I have no idea what she is on about.

'Your so-called friend Jude is slagging you all over Facebook'

'She is doing what?!'

I am shocked, even for Jude this is low.

I didn't expect her to agree with me when I told her about Tylor, but I honestly didn't think she would slag me off online, is she really that childish?

'She is telling whoever will listen that you are a, please excuse my language, but a slag who meets up with random men in hotels'

I could fucking, kill that woman, how dare she.

'Well Tylor is far from random, I will kill her Carrie' I snap not meaning to shoot the messenger.

'Don't lower yourself to her level Ella, she has done it to get a reaction, just delete the post and block her. I am sure that will piss her off a hell of a lot more'

Carrie has a point and I am not sure how things would turn out if I did come to blows with Jude.

I can throw a dig, but Jude is at least double my weight and is almost a foot taller than me. She would more than likely kick my arse.

Before blocking Jude, I look at her newsfeed.

She really is pissed; every meme is about betrayal and loyalty. Honestly, she looks like she is just trying to get attention and then I see the status Carrie was telling me about. It is a bit long winded to read it out, but it basically says how she knows someone who would rather give up her friends and family just to get laid. A bit over dramatic if you ask me. I need to stop myself from commenting on the post, I know if I do, I will just cause myself even more aggravation. So, I just hit the block button.

I message Carrie and tell her I have blocked Jude and arrange to meet up with her tomorrow to tell her about my night away. At least someone is happy for me.

Being annoyed has me cleaning this place in record time and as I sit on the bed with a coffee and a book. I notice it is only just gone three in the afternoon.

I really should go out for a walk, but I honestly cannot be bothered; so, a day of reading and writing poetry is in order.

My stomach starts to grumble, and I realize that I haven't eaten anything today. I peel, myself off the bed and make my way to the fridge, but it is bare and unless I fancy living on noodles I really need to get some shopping in. Feeling frustrated I put my shoes on and save what little bit of writing I have managed so far.

My head is all over the place, what with Jude and her reaction but also because I half expected a message from Tylor today and he hasn't.

I want to message him, but at the same time I know he has a life and I don't want to seem too keen and scare him away. I know I will end up ranting about how shitty my day has been so far: so, it is probably best if leave him be. With that in mind I place my phone on the bed and head out the door. It needs to charge anyway so I decide to leave it at home.

Shopping in these big supermarkets late afternoon seems crazy now that I am here, the place is busy, and I don't have the energy to stand around waiting in the cue.

The woman in front of me keeps sneezing and the rude part of me wants to tell her to cover her mouth.

You can literally see the germs escaping, yet both her hands remain, on the trolley in front of her.

You have got to be kidding me!

Now they have just closed the till and are redirecting me to the other line, I am going be here all night at this rate.

Finally, I am served, by the untidiest teenage I have ever seen. What is it with people today, does no one have any care, for what they look like in public?

He could have at least washed his hands, they are covered in pen and some yellow staining. I don't even want to try and guess what it is.

I think I have seen it all when I walk outside, and the local drunk is throwing up beside the bin.

This all seems like a lot of hassle just for a few bits and pieces for the fridge and as you can imagine, food is the last thing on my mind now.

I am almost ready for bed when my phone rings. It's Tylor.

'Good evening darling, how's you?' he asks.

Now I could go on a big rant and tell him about my entire day, but I just tell him, that it has been one of them days.

My mood improves as we are chatting away for ages; I do end up telling him about my horrid shopping experience and he laughs at my misfortune, he also tells me how I should have said something to the sneezing old lady and that he wouldn't be surprised if I have a raging cold in a few days. It's funny I don't think I could ever get tired of hearing his voice. Our conversation is flowing, and I find it so easy to listen to him. Then the phone goes deadly quiet, and I realize he is slowly falling asleep, as if I have bored him that much, he is falling asleep while still on the phone to me.

'I should let you get some sleep' I whisper.

'No, I am wide awake' he says, although it is clear he isn't. his voice is soft and sleepy, and I can tell his eyes are closed.

'Goodnight darling, I will talk to you tomorrow'

'Ni night sweetheart'

I hang up the phone and lay in the dark room looking up at the shadows on the ceiling.

I am on cloud nine as I drift off to sleep.

I dreamt about Tylor for what felt like most of the night. He seriously is on my mind twenty-four seven and it is driving me a little crazy. My dream was quite normal; we are both sat in the back seat of a taxi and Tylor is telling me all about his teenage years and all the things he used to get up to on the streets of Belfast growing up; which only makes me realize how little I know about him, in real life.

I think I like this air of mystery though and Tylor really doesn't seem like the type of man to talk about his past in detail. He is quite a secretive man, whereas I am the complete opposite. I am not as bad nowadays but there was a time that all you needed to do was feed me alcohol and I would tell you my whole life story.

Now, I only talk about things if someone asks me.

Its only eight thirty in the morning but now that I am awake I may as well get up and take a shower. My dream was very plutonic, but I have woken up horny as anything and can't wait to feel the water trickling down my body.

It looks like it might be a lovely day today, so I fetch out a dress and underwear.

As soon as the water hits off my naked body my nipples start to harden, and I can feel my insides clench as the water makes it way down my body, creating a small waterfall from my groin.

I find myself rubbing the bubbles from the shower gel all over my chest, spending extra time circling my now hardened nipples. I would never have touched my tiny breasts before. The water trails down my body and meets with my stomach. It sends a shiver within my body.

'Oh fuck!' I gasp as I tighten my grip on breasts.

After pulling hard on my nipple with the other hand and using the now spare hand to tease my lady bits again. I instantly feel my legs tighten as I push my fingers inside myself. I can hardly take it as my legs start to go weak, they shake as I reach my climax, letting out a long moan.

Just the thought of Tylor turns me on and I am far from complaining. I have never known of a man having so much control, without being in my company.

CHAPTER TWENTY THREE…

Life seems really boring lately and I need something to brighten up my mood and give me something to look forward to, so I message Tylor and ask him if he fancy's some company at the end of the month. We have already agreed to meet up again and I did offer to go and see him in Cardiff before he comes to visit me. I think part of him must still be annoyed from the last time he tried to visit me, and I can't blame him.

Tylor replies almost straight away and said he had been thinking the same thing so, after our brief phone call, I get online and start searching for tickets. I am pleasantly surprised when I see the prices and book my trip to the south of Wales for two weeks-time.

I message Tylor to tell him that I have my tickets booked and he replies with happy emoji's. I know he is busy at work, so I leave it till the evening before talking to him again. Tylor seems almost as excited as me that I will be staying with him. I have an open return, but we plan to spend Friday evening through to Sunday together. It will be the longest we have been in each-others company and I do worry that he will get bored of me after a few days.

Not that I think I am boring, it is just that Tylor is hard to read at times and very unpredictable when it comes to what he says.

I am so excited that we have a plan in action now and I honestly cannot wait to see him again. I hear Cardiff is beautiful this time of year and I just hope the warm sunny weather continues, while I am down there. Tylor has sent me a few photos of where he lives to give me an idea on the type of activities he has in mind for us.

I don't care what we do, as long as I am in his company, I know I will be smiling the whole time.

Even if we stay indoors I know this trip will be epic.

Tylor has assured me that we will be out just as much as we are indoors and told me to pack a decent pair of walking shoes.

I didn't want to say that I don't own a pair, but I give myself a mental note that I need to buy myself some trainers or something at the end of the week.

Mum has just text me, so I decided to ring her instead, I am all excited as I tell her my plans and Mum tells me how happy she is for me. Once I am off the phone I decide an early night is in order.

It is only quarter past ten at night, but I am done in.

CHAPTER TWENTY FOUR…

This past two weeks have flown in quick enough, although I was bored shitless all last week.

Tomorrow I am travelling down to Cardiff and I am packing my bag this morning because I want to make sure I have everything I need. I am stupidly excited and have Carrie coming to stay tonight to keep me company and to also make sure I am up on time. My alarm hasn't woken me the past few mornings and even though my train isn't until late morning I don't want to take anything to chance.

I am only staying for a few days, but I have taken extra clothes just in case we go out. Tylor has told me that we will be doing a lot of walking over the weekend, so I got myself a pair of trainers. Sounds good to me because I love nothing more than to be outdoors and surrounded by nature. Plus, Tylor has hinted that he wants us to be intimate outdoors and again I am happy enough with that but worry that we may get caught in the act.

Tylor seems to be bringing out my more daring side and I am liking it a lot.

Carrie got here just before seven and I can tell I am doing her head in always talking about Tylor, but I am excited and slightly nervous about seeing him again.

Before I met him I honestly didn't have any excitement in my life, I felt like my dull boring existence had sucked most of the life out of me.

Tylor makes my blood pump and you know that saying about how if someone or something can make you feel alive, you should run with it.

I think I have finally clicked onto what they mean.

I smile far too much, and I get nervous as hell around him but in the same breath no man has ever made me feel as comfortable about myself as I am when I am around him.

'Can you please talk about something else?' she asks playfully but I can see I am frustrating her.

Carrie has been in an on, off relationship with the same guy for over four years and when they are good she is on cloud nine, but when they have had a falling out like they have done this week, Carrie is a shadow of herself and it is horrible to see. The last thing she needs is me raving on about my love life.

I get my guitar out and we have a little sing while it is still early. Tylor messages me about ten-ish as soon as he has finished work every night this week, so I plan to put the guitar away before then anyway.

Carrie is a little tipsy which seems funny because we have only had two glasses of rum but then again, she doesn't drink that often.

I take my phone call at twenty past ten and Tylor knows that I have Carrie sat with me, so he purposely starts talking dirty down the phone. He tells me how he is looking forward to all the diverse ways he is going to please me, and that his bedroom will be soaked in my juices before the weekend is up.

I have no doubt in my mind that he will stay true to his word and I can feel my body start to take notice.

Tylor knows for a fact that I can't say anything back, I don't want to rub Carrie's face in it and I get a little embarrassed when I try and talk dirty.

I can send a naughty text but that is as far as it goes.

I go to bed feeling a little frustrated sexually but even if I didn't have Carrie sleeping in my bed beside me, I still would be just as frustrated because Tylor has told me I am not allowed to touch myself until I see him tomorrow.

He is a cheeky sod though because while he is forbidding me for pleasing myself, he has his cock in his hand and sending me short videos of him masturbating. I'm not really complaining though as all this sexual frustration just adds to the electrical chemistry between us. I still manage to fall asleep with a big smile on my face.

The next morning, I wake up before either Carrie's or my own alarms have had chance to go off.

You can tell I am excited I think to myself as I make my way to the bathroom to run my bath. I then make my way down the stairs to make Carrie and myself a coffee.

My friend is best not spoken to until she has had her coffee and a smoke.

I feel a little sick, but I haven't eaten yet and I am so excited about seeing him later that I doubt I will be able to eat anything.

Carrie is being a pain in the arse and refusing to get up, but I need to get this room sorted out before I start getting ready, so I head down the stairs and blast the music on.

I am sure the neighbours hate me as it isn't even ten in the morning, but I need my mate out of bed, so I can get dressed in peace. I am stood in just a towel and it isn't the warmest of mornings.

Ten minutes later I have my bedroom back to myself.

I am just putting my trousers on when Tylor calls me to make sure we are still on for today.

As if I am going to change my mind, I cannot wait to see him. I tell him that I will text when I am on my way and he informs, me that he was working late last night so is heading back to bed for an hour.

I am at the platform half an hour early; can you tell I am keen? Tylor has messaged me to say that he will meet me at the train station just after two. He knows my train is due in at ten past the hour.

Two hours later I arrive in London and need to get on the next train to Cardiff. I have sent Tylor a text to tell him I should be with him within the next hour or so.

Once in Cardiff the nervous butterflies turn to worry as Tylor is nowhere to be seen. I have walked the platforms twice and even headed into the coffee shop to see if I can see him. I start to worry because I have tried to ring him three times, but his phone is just ringing out.

I am hoping he is on his way, so I decide rather than worrying myself into an unneeded headache I decide to grab a coffee and ring my Mum. She always has the best advice.

'Hello love' she answers chirpy.

'Mummy I have a problem'

I go on to explain that I am in Cardiff and unfortunately Tylor is nowhere to be seen. She asked me why I don't just knock on his door and I inform her that I foolishly don't have his address.

I little bit of de ja vu don't you think?

'Do you think this is his way of getting back at you for standing him up last time Ella?' Mum asks and now that she has mentioned it, I am starting to think that it is.

'Would be just my luck' I sigh.

I really hope that, it isn't the case, but at the same time I do kind of deserve it if he does stand me up.

'Well you have already paid for you tickets, you can either, go back home, or find a lovely hotel and spend a few days away. Go and treat yourself for a change' she says.

'I'm not sure, let me ring him back and see if he picks up this time'

We say our goodbyes and I promise my Mum that I will let her know what happens.

I finish drinking my coffee before rolling a cigarette and making my way outside. I try to ring Tylor again and I hope to God he picks up this time, because if not I will be getting the next train home.

I know my Mum said about staying in Cardiff but the thought of being here, on my own, has me a little on edge.

The phone is ringing but still no response. It is coming up to three o clock now and I have been here for just under an hour. I am giving him another half an hour before I am calling it a day. I really hope he answers his fucking phone, because I am starting to feel like the April fool for sure, even if it is the start of May.

I ring him again. 'please answer the phone' I beg.

TO MY READERS...

This story may be a little different to the genre that I would normally write, and I hope you have enjoyed reading this book, just as much as I enjoyed making it...

Will Tylor answer his phone, or will he even turn up?

Ella is feeling very on edge and doesn't like being in a place she doesn't know at the best of times. With Tylor, not reachable, she is starting to wonder if this was part of his game all along...

Find out what happens in book two of 'The Ella and Tylor Story' I hope I have intrigued you enough to follow their love story a little further....

SR xoxo

A simple hello, is never that simple...

25264144R00139

Printed in Poland
by Amazon Fulfillment
Poland Sp. z o.o., Wrocław